Anne Fine is a distinguished children's writer who has won the Carnegie medal twice, the Whitbread Children's Award twice, the *Guardian* Children's Literature Award and a Smarties Prize. An adaptation of her novel *Goggle-Eyes* has been shown by the BBC and Twentieth Century Fox filmed her novel *Madame Doubtfire* as *Mrs Doubtfire*, starring Robin Williams.

Anne Fine has written four adult novels: *The Killjoy*, *Taking the Devil's Advice*, which was adapted for radio, *In Cold Domain* and *Telling Liddy*. She has two grown-up daughters and lives in County Durham.

Also by Anne Fine

TAKING THE DEVIL'S ADVICE
IN COLD DOMAIN
TELLING LIDDY

THE KILLJOY

Anne Fine

BLACK SWAN

THE KILLJOY
A BLACK SWAN BOOK : 0 552 99828 1

Originally published in Great Britain by Bantam Press,
a division of Transworld Publishers Ltd

PRINTING HISTORY
Bantam Press edition published 1986
Penguin edition published 1994
Black Swan edition published 1999

1 3 5 7 9 10 8 6 4 2

Set in 11pt Garamond by
County Typesetters, Margate, Kent

Black Swan Books are published by Transworld Publishers Ltd,
61–63 Uxbridge Road, London W5 5SA,
in Australia by Transworld Publishers,
c/o Random House Australia Pty Ltd,
20 Alfred Street, Milsons Point, NSW 2061,
in New Zealand by Transworld Publishers,
c/o Random House New Zealand,
18 Poland Road, Glenfield, Auckland
and in South Africa by Transworld Publishers,
c/o Random House (Pty) Ltd,
Endulini, 5a Jubilee Road, Parktown 2193.

Reproduced, printed and bound in Great Britain by
Cox & Wyman Ltd, Reading, Berks.

For my patron

THE KILLJOY

Chapter 1

Now it's all over I can tell about it – not dispassionately, you understand; but without passion. I feel myself again, careful and middle-aged, and if you were to interrupt me I'd listen thoughtfully to what you had to say and probably nod my head along with you as if this were just another seminar, saying, 'Quite so. Quite so.'

I hadn't realized that I used that particular phrase so often. Nor was I accustomed to being teased about the way I talk. I generally don't invite that kind of derision. I am a quiet man, a deliberate man. I think before I speak and I don't speak often. I'm not a rattler like a lot of my colleagues. I come in carrying my briefcase at half past nine each morning. I try not to let my correspondence bank up. I start my lectures promptly on the hour. I eat my sandwich and apple early, at my desk, to save time. In so far as administrative commitments allow, I keep the afternoons free for my own work, arranging seminars and appointments with students as far as possible for four o'clock or even later. Slotted into the day in this fashion they make a reasonable break and mean that by the time I've reached home and cooked my supper, with luck I'm ready to pick up work again. I might get three or four more hours in before I take the newspaper to bed. I've lived my life in this unflurried way right from the day my marriage ended. Indeed, my ex-wife Margaret claims that the marriage ended partly because I lived my life in this way beforehand as well.

The day you're asking about was in no way unusual, you understand. Nothing of any significance happened until that late afternoon seminar began to fall apart. There were five of us present. Who? Let me see. Well, Davie, as you keep calling her, of course. Warner, MacFaddyen, McKinley and myself. Scott-Watson should have been there but he was sick, or said he was. It was McKinley's essay we were discussing, and I was sitting quietly and comfortably behind my desk whilst McKinley defended himself at quite unwarrantable length against some small criticism that had been levelled at one of his slighter points. For all our sakes, I was watching for an opportunity to cut him off and, seizing one moment as good as any, I interrupted.

'Quite so. Quite so.'

She made a tiny noise – yes, her. She made this little noise, the oddest sound, a sort of soft popping explosion at the back of her throat. Naturally I took it for a sneeze, and rose to pull the window down. The minute my back was turned, McKinley began to remake his really very

10

tedious point and so I said again, rather more sharply:

'Quite so. Quite so.'

When I looked round again, her shoulders were shaking. I saw them. There she sat, in her scruffy blue jeans and pretty flowered blouse, trying not to laugh. There's not so much merriment goes on in Comparative Government II that I didn't notice.

Allowing McKinley a few last moments in which to crash on through his undergrowth of constitutional trivia, I raised a warning eyebrow at her. She took a deep breath, but all that happened was that her eyes began to shine more dangerously with the effort. Best way to quell most students is to ask them a question, so:

'I'm interested, Alicia, in your opinion of Stuart's wee point.'

No, that's not unusual. I call them all by their first names. I have for years. I think most of us do these days, you know. Indeed, I recall reading in some teaching manual that it unwinds them, makes them that tiny bit more forthcoming in discussion. Not that it worked in this case. She only pulled herself together sufficiently to manage a sort of strangled cough.

Once you've started in you have to persist or all the rest begin to think they too will get away with squeaks and grunts and so forth. I didn't want to be a killjoy but this is a university, you know. We do have aims and standards.

'Alicia?'

Her eyes were still more than usually bright, her cheeks pink, but she took another breath and did her best. 'I suppose he's right. I just don't think it's at all important

11

compared with all that other stuff we've gone through.'

I said it without thinking.

'Quite so. Quite so.'

All the amusement she'd been so strenuously banking up inside her exploded. No soft discreet poppings of merriment this time, no barely discernible shaking of shoulders. She had to fight for breath, she was laughing so hard. Her eyes glistened and filled. Her whole body shook. We all stared at her, but she couldn't stop. She struggled with herself, tears streaming down her face, becoming weaker and weaker, until it became clear even to her that she was quite helpless. She bowed her head to try to excuse herself, and all that happened was that her shoulders shook more violently. She put up her hands to hide her face and tears spurted through between her fingers. Then the poor thing at last gave up. Letting her hands fall into her lap, and sitting there quite blinded with tears, she laughed and laughed at me. No, I didn't mind. Why on earth should I? I'd seen she'd done her very best not to start in the first place and, once that failed, to stop again. She'd tried to help herself. She simply couldn't.

The rest of us, we were reduced to mesmerized attendance. McKinley grinned, if a little ruefully. The stupid laddie still supposed that she was laughing at him. The others smiled, polite and patient. But me, I simply stared at her. You'll find this difficult to believe, perhaps, but I had, till that moment, completely forgotten just how it feels to be pleased by another human being. Is that unusual? I can't speak for others. All I know is that for the first time in many, many years – it felt, as I sat watching her, as if it might be for the first time ever – I was delighted. She had delighted me.

What happened then? I passed across the box of paper tissues. I always keep one on the bookshelf. There's generally someone with a heavy cold, or hay fever. Women occasionally burst into tears. You're familiar with the term *in loco parentis*. Well, that's about all it amounts to at this stage, handing out tissues. McKinley chivalrously uprooted a couple, one pink and one green, and pushed them into her limp hand and she began to mop as I picked up the first of four crucial issues McKinley, in his essay, had failed to air, I won't say discuss, and if you'd read as much as I have of McKinley's work, you'd understand my reluctance.

I questioned. I waited hopefully. I answered myself as concisely and illuminatingly as I could, doing the job I'm paid for, trying to prod the lardy lumps into a bit of real thought; and that's how we went on, me taking up the issues, her the tissues. She wiped and blotted and dabbed, and blew her pretty little nose. And when she was at last recovered, she had the grace to lift her face and let her hair fall back so I could see for myself that she was now prepared to rejoin us.

'Better?'

'Better.'

She smiled. She thought she was secure, you understand. I'm a kind enough man, and she was content, after her few brief moments of treating me as if I were fully human, to put me back up on the distant shelf on which people like her prefer to keep people like me. But she'd delighted me so much that I did something

13

unprecedented in all my years of teaching. I cruelly and deliberately presented her with what she'd always been so careful to avoid, sitting tucked there upon the left side of the door, always arriving early so she'd be sure to get the safest seat, scooting out first the moment we drew to a close. I slowly and steadily swivelled my chair round and gave her a smile, my best smile. Pinned her down with it, you might almost say. The poor thing, through one brief lapse of courtesy, was momentarily in thrall to me. She couldn't simply lower or avert her eyes as she had always done before, as everybody does, as you yourself did when you first came in and introduced yourself and started asking all these questions. For once, she had no choice but to submit. I turned and showed her the bad side of me, the ghastly and disfigured part of me, this ugly no-go area, this scar patch on my face.

This scar here, this one with the worst puckering that runs through all the others, it's eighteen inches long. When I first measured, it was only thirteen and a half. It's grown along with me. I measured accurately, I assure you, using a length of thread, tracking it round all the bends as if it were a cycling distance on a country map. If you count this line here, this one, as the main scar and follow it down here instead of down there, that makes it twenty-two and a quarter inches long because this runnel goes down even deeper. It rises the same two and three-quarter inches above my hairline, clearly; but it goes down four and a bit farther under my collar. The worst of it, believe it or not, is out of sight – except that, being out of sight, it's not the worst of it. The rich colour is the most unpleasant thing for people, I often think. That, more than the actual lumping and scarring itself, upsets them. In some lights, garish coloured lights that disguise the lividness a little, I almost might simply be scowling horribly. Once, in a hotel room with some strange fuzzy blue light flashing outside, I thought for a moment, catching sight of that side of myself in the mirror, that I was just some surly porter passing the doorway.

It is a great shame, yes. No, don't apologize. I realize you didn't mean it in that sense, but shame is the right word. It is a shame. Seen from one side, I am as pleasant-looking as the next man. Seen from the other, I am repellent. It is a shame and that is how I carry it. I find I walk down the right-hand side of staircases. I hug the right-hand wall along a corridor. I stand close to the right-hand side of a lift. I even realized, a few months ago, that the dentist to whom I've gone for years is left-handed! Now you could say that was coincidence, but frankly I doubt it. In the same ward as me, where they first tried to patch me up, there was a little girl with one eye higher in her head than the other. She was a tiny little thing. I look back now and I would say she cannot have been more than two years old. Already she was tilting her head casually and coquettishly to one side whenever she talked to anyone, whenever she noticed anybody looking at her, so that, although she didn't ever look quite right, you couldn't tell at a glance what was wrong. Eighteen months old. Two at the most. Don't try to tell me I walk right across the city to a left-handed dentist by chance.

You'll be curious about how it happened. Everyone is, though they don't ask. As I walk down the aisles of supermarkets I hear little voices pipe up till their hands

15

are warningly squeezed. It's always 'Why—?' Or 'How—?' Adults are more restrained, of course. Women will only ask if we're alone and there's no chance of our being interrupted whilst I 'talk about it'; a man doesn't ask unless we've downed at least three pints together and there's another in his hand – one of the reasons I now drink in such moderation. It all still boils down to How and When and Why. I'll tell you how and when, they're simple enough.

When I was five years old I tangled with next door's Alsatian. And such a lasting mess from that sort of encounter was common enough back then, too. Not like these days, when people practically stroll along to casualty, their severed parts tucked under their arms, and queue to have them sewn back on. I shouldn't be bitter, though. The poor Alsatian did far worse. He got put down. And that breed is supposed to be intelligent. So that's the How and When of it. But as for Why, I can't begin to guess, and anyway, that's the next corridor along, Why. Quite a distinguished department, I'm told.

I speak facetiously, of course. Philosophers don't think about that kind of thing these days. They're far too high-powered. I do, though. I've thought about it from time to time and told myself that everyone could be luckier than they end up, that one is fortunate to gain some satisfaction from one or two of the few things that aren't randomly denied by genetics or upbringing, society or chance. So what's a mangled half of a face? I ask myself. Some people on whom it doesn't show are just as deeply scarred as I am. One day I might be argon-lasered into a Gregory Peck, but they'll never get to go the ways they haven't gone from ignorance or stupidity. In any case, the only thing I ever envied anyone was being treated as a human being.

My saying that makes you uneasy, doesn't it? You must, in your profession, have heard the foulest things, seen the worst sights. What you found at my flat this morning is nothing to some of them, I'll be bound. And yet this is the second time that what I've said has made you uncomfortable. Is that your guilt? I think it is. You know I'm right. Nobody treats a man as disfigured as I am as if he were human. Colleagues are irreproachably courteous in discussion. Strangers turn out of their road to show me mine. My students even hand their work in on time! You'll not believe this, but in sixteen years of marriage my wife never once turned on me and snapped, 'Oh, go away! I'm sick of the sight of you!' I've struggled in a swamp of courtesy and consideration since I was five years old, and I'm still sucked down in it now, more than forty years later. Even you, you've become a part of it. You strode in here after the most peremptory of knocks and, though you'd bet your index-linked pension that I was wholly responsible for what you saw up in my flat, because my sheer hideousness took you by surprise, because you had to make that effort not to flinch when I looked up, your whole manner changed. You came in to arrest a man like yourself, and you encountered me instead. Instantly you became like everybody else, as steady and as courteous as a rock.

Rocks. That's what the world's been filled with for me, you understand. Rocks, not people. It's all been rocks, one rock after another. Even my ex-wife, the kindest and most generous-spirited rock you could meet, willing herself not to see the ugly side of me so she could see through to the rest. Oh, admirable. But it didn't work. We were only half married – the pleasant-looking half.

So since my marriage to Margaret became unravelled, I've not really taken too much interest in women. I lived alone and read the newspaper until Alicia Davie laughed in my face for all the world as if she had forgotten about the other side of it, the side she couldn't see from where she was sitting. I turned the ugly side of me on her more just to get it over with than for any other reason. She'd made me feel not just good but real, happy almost. But she was bound to slip away again like everyone else. The longer I warmed to her, the worse for me. You could just say I was simply giving her a cue to withdraw.

I think, to be fair, I overdid it. I made my eyes rounder than usual, staring, a bit demented. I puffed my bad cheek up with air. Horrid, yes? I gave her the works. I swung round on her like this. See?

She gasped again but not like she had before, not from laughter. She jumped to her feet. She slapped my cheek so hard she almost knocked me out of my chair.

'*Bully!*'

The faces of the others turned to masks. Nobody moved. Nobody spoke. All I heard was my own sharp intake of breath. Scar tissue isn't the most sensitive, but still it stung like hell. I put one hand up to my face to hold the pain, the other out, without thinking. I laid it on her arm to steady her, so she would not run out on me.

'I'm sorry,' I told her.

'I hope it hurt!'

18

'It did. It did.'

'Well, you deserved it!'

'Oh, yes,' I said, 'I deserved it.' And then, to try to keep from falling on my knees at her feet in front of them all, I soothed us both as best as I could, muttering, 'Quite so. Quite so.'

I walked back home across the park. Generally I find I spend this period of time reviewing my day, thinking back over the brief conversations I've had with my colleagues, the lectures I've given, administrative meetings at which I've been present. I think about what I feel like eating or, more to the point, what I feel like cooking for supper. The things I have to do the next day run through my mind: papers to mark, references to check, articles to root out from the library. I tend not to consider my own research on this short walk. I find I need a more sustained period of quiet, fewer visual distractions, if I'm to think about that to advantage. I value this time of day. If I encounter anyone I know approaching me from the opposite direction, I'll stop and chat briefly; but if I see I'm setting off at the same time as a colleague, I'll first establish which of the several paths across the park he's planning to take, and then set off down another. And if I notice I'm walking fast enough to catch up with anyone I recognize from the back, I'll tend to slow my pace until I reach the next fork in the path, and then I'll take the other way. I need these minutes of reflection. I don't know how others get through their day without them. I know there are those who can usher out their last students, steer a colleague aside in the corridor for a hasty discussion, run for a crowded city bus, leap off outside a day-care centre to pick up a son or a daughter, listen to its chatter all the way home, and still greet the rest of their family with equanimity. But I'm not like that and I never have been. I am a quiet man and I need quiet. That's not to say that Margaret and I didn't discuss the notion of having a family; and had I myself been keener, she would no doubt have gone ahead and braved it. But, looking back, I think it just as well I laid no claim to abilities I'm quite convinced I neither have nor could have easily developed. I find all children a bit of a strain, to be truthful. I speak to them civilly enough, usually if they address me first, but I find conversation with them awkward. I don't know what they're interested in, and can't readily attune myself to whichever level of understanding they've reached. To be frank, I don't at all comprehend the way that their minds work. I'll see a child in pigtails, apparently absorbed in the *Beano*, and five minutes later she'll lift her head to inform her father of the projected effects of a five-megaton bomb falling on Kirknewton. Parents seem able to divine which areas of their offspring's mind are reasonably well developed, and which are still hopelessly retarded. It's all a mystery to me. I find the very idea of living in the same house as a child exhausting. I'm glad I had the sense to see and accept this aspect of myself from the start; though I do regret for Margaret's sake that by the time we finally parted she was really a little too old to have the option of becoming a mother. But, as I've said, life is a series of things denied, for one accidental reason after another. There's nothing to be done about that.

Yes, I walk to work and back through the worst of weather. I have no car. I use the tree-lined footpath across the centre of the park whenever it's raining, as it gives a little more protection than the less sheltered pathways. I never use the bus. I thoroughly dislike travelling in buses. They're packed with schoolchildren at my times of day, and I find their covert glances at my face unnerving. I could lash out on a taxi from time to time, I suppose, but I've always preferred routine to comfort or convenience. The more closely each of my days mirrors the one before, the more contented I am. And that's no doubt why I found it so disquieting, that afternoon, to stride along between the trees as usual, yet find that, unusually, one thing was on my mind the whole time. I'd expected to think about it a bit. It was a part of my day. It had happened. I'd quite unpredictably made a hideous face at a student, and she had slapped it. That kind of thing is not the norm in Comparative Government II. Naturally, walking home, I'd find myself reflecting on the incident, and that in itself did not surprise me. What did was that I wasn't really thinking about the slap itself. I felt almost at ease about that. It was, after all, she who had slapped me, and not what would have given me far more pause for thought – I who had slapped her. That, given my position in the university, could have meant nothing short of disaster. No, what bothered me was that I was no longer so much thinking about the incident itself as about Alicia Davie: who she was, where she lived, and why she laughed at me.

Make no mistake, I'm not in the habit of brooding about my female students. I don't, to be honest, find very many of them attractive. I see their beauty and their health and their occasional grace, yes; nevertheless, there's always something about them that douses all flickers of interest – mostly their youth. They wear it like a shield and, under pressure, it doubles as an offensive weapon. This is some hangover from childhood and school, I have no doubt; but as I'm neither a parent nor a schoolmaster, their youth is none of my concern and I don't care to have it thrust under my nose or tacitly offered to me as an excuse. I don't choose to be subjected to either their giddy high spirits or their exaggerated fears and woes. I simply want to see the paper I asked them to write on *Constitutional Changes in Spain since 1931* sitting in my pigeon-hole by four o'clock on the day I specified.

This may sound churlish, but I'm not as isolated in these sentiments as you might imagine. 'Anderson – what's he like?' someone will enquire over the tea trolley. 'Young,' comes the pained reply, and we all nod. Youth can't be helped, but it could be far better hidden. Once, in the corridor, I came across Brown getting shirty with two female students. 'I just left two hulking daughters batting their eyelashes at me because they hadn't done the washing up. I don't need you two to start batting yours because you haven't finished that essay.' He did apologize almost at once, but the young ladies stalked off in a huff all the same.

And just as Brown is no easy prey for batting eyelashes, I have stood firm in the face of tears and pleas and thinly veiled threats of self-inflicted harm. I've held out against more excuses than you could imagine, to the extent of keeping a list in my desk of the funerals attended by each of my students. You'd be surprised to learn how often someone's maternal granny tries to die twice around here. Like Brown, I'm not a soft man and I can't be hood-winked or beguiled. I'm not used to walking home across the park in a fret, letting my supper burn under the grill and finding the newspaper I've been saving all day little short of tedious. I'm not used to seeing over and over in my mind's eye a pretty face gone solemn with the effort of trying not to laugh at me. It made me tense, irritable even; and it was late before I fell asleep.

In the morning for the first time in my life that I remember, I cut my finger slicing the heel off a loaf of bread. I watched the blood soak into what should by right have been my breakfast and cursed Alicia Davie out loud for a witch. On the way into work, on less of an impulse than I care to admit, I dropped into the Administration Office to look up her file. Her full name was Alicia Anna Davie. Her year of birth bore the current nightmare penultimate digit – was, in fact, 1965. In 1965 I'd been a steadily married man for nine years – small wonder that they call us 'Wrinklies'. Her file gave two addresses. In term time she lived at 18A Ardmory Road, in the city: but she had entered as her home address Brightmony, Brightmony. For a moment I wondered whether, in some fit of absent-mindedness, she'd written Brightmony twice over in error: but the care of the hand-writing and spacing, and the comma between, belied that notion. I turned the page. All her examination results were creditable, and her school references were excellent. In fact, she wasn't to be faulted on paper and, Lord knows, I stood there long enough trying.

Over the next two weeks I progressed steadily from thinking about her a good deal to thinking about her most of the time. I kept up with my teaching, but, in between times, my own work fell apart at the seams. Unanswered letters, unread papers gathered on my desk. The secretaries and the cleaning ladies looked askance at these rising piles of clutter, but I simply rested my head and arms upon them and, bearing only her in mind, cradled my fast-spawning thoughts to the exclusion of everything else. Researches into Brown's tattered copy of *Scotland's for Me* revealed that, as I suspected, Brightmony was an hotel, or, rather, a guest-house. (Props: Mr & Mrs Alasdair Davie. Set in magnificent countryside excellent for fishing (salmon and trout), bird-watching, hill-walking and mountain-climbing, and offering four bedrooms, each with hot & cold, central heating. Lounge and TV. Fire certificate. Ample private parking. Quality home baking.) Apart from these small glimpses into the domestic arrangements of her home and the scenic and recreational attractions of her locality, I knew almost nothing about her. Still I would find myself ridiculously wondering whether, out there at 18A Ardmory Road, she missed her mother's quality home baking; ludicrously wanting to know if she had brought her hill-walking shoes along with her for these term-time weeks of city living behind the coal depot and the roller-skating rink; insanely anxious lest she was home-sick, longing for Brightmony, its burns and quarries, its bogs and cart-tracks.

I grant you, I became obsessed. Still, in our seminars I

behaved impeccably, handing back her papers with the same courteous detached gravity that I accord to Warner, MacFaddyen, McKinley and even Scott-Watson, whenever he's present. No-one would ever have guessed that I was burning inside. Caught staring at her pale bare arms one afternoon, I casually asked if she didn't feel chilly. On the day she appeared with black and gold fingernails, I made no remark. Once, only once, did I allow myself a luxury – that of expressing some small disquiet over the quality of her essay comparing the role of the judiciary in the American and British political systems.

'Not so good,' I warned gently. 'I trust you'll find some of my written comments helpful.'

She shuddered a little.

'Give it some thought over the next few days, would you?'

'Yes,' she said. 'No. I suppose so. I might.'

Extraordinary.

I nodded, as though her incoherence made perfect sense, and let her go off with the others with no more than the customary goodbye.

As the door closed behind them, and the echoes of their exaggerated groans of relief died away in the corridor outside, I laid my head down on my books and papers, and I gave in. I crumpled. I faced the fact that I, Ian James Laidlaw, Professor, three days from turning forty-nine years old, a calm, good teacher set fair for uneventful retirement followed by uneventful old age and uneventful death, had now defected from my former self, had turned turtle for a pretty face, and that, for all that I could tell, there was no getting back. Can I express to you the horror? Better not. But you can understand the shame. I have a deal of knowledge and experience, age and some wisdom. If you'd been present on that afternoon, brought out your Penguin *Freud* and started to explain myself to me, I would have interrupted you at once: 'Quite so. Quite so. I know. I know.' For I knew everything, except what to do. And no-one could have told me that.

Chapter 2

It would be hard to argue that I followed her, exactly. Generally, yes, I do go directly home, but not always. I had a number of things to do on that side of the city. I had a pair of trousers to pick up from Mrs McEwen who does my sewing repairs for me. I wanted to ask at Filmer's whether they stocked a particular type of door lock. I've ordered from the coal depot in that street before.

I caught up with her at the end of Junction Street, before she turned off into Ardmory Road. The woolly hat whose myriad holes she spent our seminar time enlarging with her fingers was jammed down hard over her ears, teapot-cosy style. The fraying ends of her drab ratty scarf trailed just below the falling hem of her coat. They look like slatterns from the back, when you can't see their bright, pretty faces. I came up on her right-hand side, slowed my brisk pace to hers, then disconcerted her by failing to speak and simply reaching out for the books she carried. Faltering, she let me take them from her. I turned them over as we walked beneath the not very penetrating orange fuzz from a street lamp, and peered at the lettering on the spines. Fitzhugh & Skidmont, Thomas Urquhart, Alasdair Mackie. She couldn't have been working on anything for me.

'Alasdair Mackie was a student of mine,' I told her. 'Years ago.'

She didn't pick me up on it. It's possible she found Mackie's book on *Scottish Nationalism* sufficiently tedious not to want to know any more, and I'd be the last to fault her for that; but I think it more likely that my sudden appearance had made her nervous. Twice, as we walked along together, she tripped, but that could have been due to the horribly run-down heels on her boots. We threaded our way through streams of children pouring, shrieking, from the roller-skating rink, she flattening herself against the high brick wall whilst I stepped out into the gutter. As I rejoined her on the first clear strip of pavement, she speeded up and kept her face averted until she reached the next kerb.

Here she stopped and faced me, reaching out for her books.

'I go down here.'

She indicated the street that stretched off behind her. I gave it a brief glance over her shoulder. Ardmory Road. Drab, mean, and very poorly lit.

'I'll walk you home.'

She shook her head and kept her hands out for the return of her books.

I added, 'As long as you don't hit me again . . .'

That went home. At least, her hands fell and she looked at me properly for the first time, embarrassed and baffled.

'Come on, then.'

I stood, stamping my feet with cold impatience whilst she glanced somewhat surreptitiously around us, fingering the holes in her horrid scarf, checking that there were others walking the streets to whom she could appeal for aid, should it prove prudent. Even the sight of several well-bundled, hurrying home-goers did not seem to reassure her.

'Alicia, I'm getting very chilly indeed, standing here.'

At last she spoke.

'About that business of my hitting you—'

I felt obliged to interrupt her.

'I find apologies very messy things. Best left unsaid, except in critical cases.'

She wasn't having that, it was clear. At once she burst out, 'It was a rotten thing to do!'

For no reason whatsoever that I can now call to mind, I took this outburst for censure of her own impropriety in slapping my face, not mine in first provoking her. I realized my mistake when, on my attempting to ease us off this really rather tiresome topic by assuring her, 'It wasn't at all important,' she positively snapped back, 'It was to *me*!'

A couple of passers-by lifted their faces from protective wads of scarves and collars in order to stare their disapproval at this young harpy bickering with her poor father on a windy street corner.

'I confess', I told her as levelly as I could, 'to feeling a shade provoked by the unpleasant turn this conversation is taking.'

'You know what you can do about that!'

And the rude little bitch swivelled on one of her shoddy, run-down boot heels and made as though to stalk off.

Now I don't live in a stationery cupboard. Though I can't claim to have been carried away by the spirit of the times, I realize that things have changed for women, and that includes the ones in British universities. Stand a female a pint at the bar these days, my male colleagues assure me, and she'd as soon sue you for sexual harassment as offer to buy you a pint in return. Better steer clear, they say. But forty-nine-year-old leopards don't change their spots so easily, and I won't stand for simple rudeness. As she turned on her heel to stride away, I dropped her library books, deliberately, in the wet gutter. Seizing her by the trailing scarf-ends, I pulled her back, hard, practically into my arms.

'Alicia Anna Davie,' I whispered, 'I've half a mind to pull this revolting scarf of yours around your neck and throttle you.' And I was close enough to watch with pleasure the shock it gave her to have the vile grooves and furrows of my face so close to hers, her rising panic at the unwelcome reminder that I, as a man, had twice her strength, her unmistakable resentment as the shade of her skin involuntarily deepened and darkened.

I know what she was thinking.

I knew what she was thinking, and I could tell you that, but not what it meant to me that she could, even for a moment, think it. Do you know, the first time that I leaned over and kissed Margaret, she was too astonished even to feel repulsion. She'd never thought of me in that way at all. People don't. And it goes deeper than that. People don't even mention certain topics in front of me, things like their loves or sexual attractions or troubles of the heart, believing, one can only presume, that to do so would be in the poorest of taste, social crassness on a par with grousing to somebody paralysed for life about one's sore feet. I am, by now, accustomed to these barriers. I take them entirely for granted. And yet, once again, she'd walked right through them. The thought had well and truly crossed her mind – I watched it – that I was following her home to rape her. You can't imagine all the tenderness and gratitude I felt towards her. Granted that she was cold and tired and no doubt somewhat overwrought; still, something entered her mind, however briefly, that would never have entered ten thousand others. Entered her mind and literally shaded her face. She'd reddened, and just the sight of it engendered in me an altogether less innocent tumescence of sensations. Hastily I stepped back from her, at once stirred and unnerved by feelings to whose arousal anywhere but in the peace and privacy of my own solitary bed I had become almost entirely a stranger. Do I sound pompous? You will, of course, be putting together your own interpretation of my account. *Got a thrill frightening the poor wee thing out of her wits*, you'll be thinking. *Went on to try and persuade himself that she was trembling in his arms for quite another reason.* You'd be quite wrong, you know. Just for the moment, sitting there, try giving me credit for some insight, some understanding. I'm sane. I'm older than you are. Possibly I'm wiser. And I tell you there was something there. Keep listening.

She wriggled to free herself and, horribly embarrassed, I let her go. She stood quietly while I loosened the scarf around her neck and draped the ends of it across her shoulders. My hands were shaking. She noticed, and I wasn't sorry. She breathed more calmly now that she realized I was harmless, simply moved. She was, all things considered, consummately well behaved, standing quite still and neither speaking nor watching my face, giving me all the time I needed to compose myself. I was grateful to her for her forbearance, and said as much.

'You must allow me to pay the full cost of replacing your library books.'

It was, to borrow the rather menacing expression of the Mafia, an offer that she couldn't refuse. She took one look at them, awash and filthied in the gutter, and she knew it. I felt a bit of a pang that any action of mine, however worthwhile in another context, should serve to boost the sales of Alasdair Mackie's appalling volume, even by one; but there was nothing to be done about that. Stooping, I fished out from the gutter Fitzhugh & Skidmont and Thomas Urquhart, parts of whom, I decided, might still be salvaged. I made a point of leaving A. Mackie sprawled, sodden, in the dirty rainwater.

Stacking the damp lump of books out of the way under one arm, I turned to her and offered her the other. Since she made no move to take it, I reached out for one of her chilled hands and tucked it neatly under my elbow.

'I realize that this is such an old-fashioned habit as to

have been entirely lost to the folk memory,' I said to her gravely, 'but everyone walked like this, back in the old days.'

Her arm relaxed a little in mine.

'What number are you?'

(As if I didn't know!)

'Eighteen.'

I peered down at the nearest little wooden gate. Forty-nine. 'Odd,' I remarked, but didn't tell her why. In any case, she had already launched into the eternal all-purpose student bleat about her lodgings, how cold her room was and how expensive, how far from the bus stop, how mean the landlord. By the time we had forced our way down the street together, arm in arm, in the teeth of a bitter wind as far as number eighteen, I had stopped listening to her entirely.

It looked, for all that I could see of it through the murk, a nasty little house, the sort of place I hadn't been in for years. You've seen it? That concrete path, almost too narrow to walk along in safety, leading past all those scruffy plants and emaciated bushes embedded in mud, and that other, even thinner, strip of concrete peeling away towards the side door. It was down this offshoot that Alicia Davie led me, stepping with all the confidence of familiarity along the rutted, ill-pitched pathway. Upstairs and down, none of the uncurtained windows was lamplit, but as my companion failed to remark on this I took it for an indication that she was accustomed to returning at night to an empty house, and wondered, not for the first time, with whom she shared it. The brick-work appeared to be slimy in the poor light from the street lamp. It looked a most unpleasant place to come home to.

You'd think I might have been prepared. There were, after all, sufficient warning signals: the neglected front garden, the face of the house, the dingy side entrance. But nothing can ever prepare one for the sheer horror of student squalor. It hits you in the face like a brick each time you see it. She flicked the light switch and there it all was. The vile, murk-coloured carpet and walls, the ill-matched sheets on the ill-made bed, the hideous posters of unshaven heroes and uncombed heroines, the light-shade made from plastic cups gleaned from some waste-bin beside a coffee-vending machine – once gleaming white, no doubt, but now an unappealing and undusted grey. Books lay all over, faces down, covers akimbo, their spines weakened beyond redemption, a bibliophile's darkest nightmare. Her clothes were scattered all about, woollens draped over the radiator, outdoor clothes piled across the back of the chair. Nests of crumpled jeans lay in the corners, and panties and socks and tights were apparently breeding everywhere, quite indiscriminately, with one another. Papers littered the floor, the shelves, the bed, the desk. Clearly she used what Brown refers to scathingly as 'an open-plan filing system'. And squatting everywhere I looked, on everything, were cups and mugs and even, I am afraid to say, jam-jars, each nursing its last inch or two of ancient, stone-cold coffee.

Oh God, the mess. My poor heart sank.

I've been appalled by this kind of thing before, of course. Glimpses at first hand, looking in briefly on student parties out of civility, dropping into the room of a sick seminar member to pick up a vital photocopy, chasing up valued personal books from sudden drop-outs. More often the horror of it has come to me second hand, as tales of squalor told over tea in the departmental office. The simple untidiness of the young people my age can learn to handle, even accept. Buttons, one knows, can be sewn on again. A good afternoon's clear-out can shift a lot of piles of clutter. But this wallowing in litter and grime of the student is quite another thing. I've seen and heard as much as the next man of these barely credible descents into slovenliness, and, apart from temporary surges of revulsion, felt very little. I've been appalled in principle, yes; but not personally shaken. Not so this time. When I looked round Alicia Davie's room. I felt more than simply upset, I felt sickened: though, to be fair, I'd have to say a good part of my repugnance stemmed from a quickening of personal shame that I should have harboured feelings for her so misplaced, so inappropriate. Surveying her room, no doubt a mirror to her habits and personality, just as my flat is mirror to mine, my private fantasy of King and Dairymaid, the Beast and Beauty, became inexorably transformed into the disagreeable reality of Dotard and Slut. I was, in an instant, quite disenchanted.

Perhaps she noticed I was looking a little bit seedy, for in an impromptu eruption of civility she offered to make me a cup of tea.

'It's only instant, though. With powdered milk.'

So she drank instant tea with powdered milk. I swear, to be that young is to be fitter than an ox. If you or I drank half a cup of that stuff, we'd feel poorly for days.

I clutched the doorway.

'You're very kind, but I had best be off.'

She might have been a little disappointed. She looked as if she might be. But just at that moment, what I had taken to be fur lining on a jacket on the armchair began to stir and stretch and yawn its way into a sleek and stripy fattish cat, and any mild desire she may have had that I should stay and take a cup of instant tea with powdered milk with her was clean forgotten in the flurry of scooping up and stroking and rubbing and welcoming. 'Brightmony, Brightmony! Pussy, puss puss!'

She'd named the cat after her home, then. And this cat was a good few years old. I stayed in the shadow of the doorway, and watched her running her fingers through his deep parting fur and tumbling him over the chair seat in pleasure, and I imagined I could see in her the child she must have been, the look she had, and even the joy it must have given her to find herself one morning the owner of a kitten, and to be able to give to it – the first of many comforting gifts of intimacy – the quite extraordinary name and address of Brightmony, Brightmony, Brightmony.

'I'll be away.'

She rose, the cat tucked in her arms.

'Good night, then.'

I stepped back into the dark of the garden and heard with relief the door close behind me. A shaft of light lit up the first few feet of the path, and I picked my way over the remainder with care. Safe under the street lamp, I turned my collar up against the night's cold, took stock, and made myself the firm and tranquillizing promise that I would never, under any circumstances, venture down Ardmory Road again.

Obsession is a wheel that spins. You can't get off it as and when you choose. Your feelings keep revolving, willy-nilly; cunning mind falls in, restless body follows, till all of you is off again, sense and perspective blurred, limbs shaking. Safe in my flat, I tip a carefully judged amount of fine tea into my grandmother's bone-china pot, and already I think myself a fool for turning down her offer of a poorly rinsed mug of vile instant tea, speckled with dehydrated milk granules. Sitting alone in my scrupulously ordered sitting-room, I envy Brightmony picking his soft-pawed way through her clutter. The monthly statement from my bank, propped on the dresser, reminds me that I live precisely within my income; and yet I bless the whim that led me only hours ago to drop a further forty pounds' worth of books into a street gutter. Am I a hopeless case? Far from it. I have begun to hope again. Before I go to bed – what for? I shan't sleep now – I draw a chair up to my writing-desk and, sliding a sheet of notepaper towards me, I start, with more care than I ever would accord any letter legitimately penned under that printed university heading, to draft the note I sent to her, the letter I have no doubt you've already found, perhaps it's in your briefcase even now, the one that begins *My Dear Miss Davie*, pretending – to her, if not to me – that it is not a simple love letter. The one that says:

My Dear Miss Davie,

Would you, for convenience' sake, come by 32 Rox-
burghe Street at six tomorrow to pick up the cheque for
your spoiled books?

Yours,
IAN LAIDLAW

At six o'clock in the evening, I thought, she couldn't
have already eaten.

But she had, or so she claimed, standing there in my
hallway, her ungloved hands blue with the cold after the
long walk from her part of the city to mine, breathless
from the stair climb. Lord knows what meal it was she
had just eaten. Very late breakfast? Not so late lunch?
Whatever it was, it probably consisted of nothing more
nourishing than cornflakes, for when she saw what I had
waiting in the kitchen her firm denial of any hunger pangs
gave way entirely. She cracked so fast, slid off her coat and
pulled a chair up to the kitchen table so promptly, I
thought it must be weeks since she had seen a slab of
good red meat lying across a chopping-board.

'How did you know I'd come?'

It did occur to me to point out that, after the first two
or three weeks of a term, bank cheques and students obey
the same natural laws of attraction as iron filings and very
strong magnets. But all I said was, 'I simply hoped.'

She watched, seemingly fascinated, as I rinsed and
peeled and chopped, making no offer to help, for which I
was inwardly grateful. I began speaking of departmental
matters, keeping the tone of everything I said as soothing

as possible, deliberately eschewing all topics vivid or controversial. I don't doubt she was even a little bored. From time to time, I slid her something across the table top, a cube of green pepper, a sliver of celery. I felt as if I were taming something: watched with a covert pleasure as she began to peer about with that burgeoning curiosity which, in the young, denotes growing ease; sensed a small flicker of achievement when she broke in upon my anodyne monologue, first to ask if the dishwasher were a washing-machine and, moments later, if the washing-machine were a dryer. She took to reaching out for titbits of food, instead of waiting for me to pass them. She fiddled with the pepper-mill, worked off its top scattering peppercorns all over, then set about retrieving every last one from her lap and the table, replacing them dutifully one by one in the little wooden tub.

I thought it safe to tempt her into conversation.

'And how are you finding Brown as a supervisor?'

'All right,' she said. 'Where did you get them?'

'The peppercorns?'

'The scars. The scars on your face. Where did you get them?'

My heart thumped, literally thumped. I stared at her across the table. Dear God, she'd done it yet again, swept the ground out from under my feet with another first. And what a first. Where? *Where?* I'm used to How? or When? but never Where? I ask you, however could I answer 'Peebles'?

'Passchendaele.'

'Oh, yes?'

She popped another titbit into her mouth, and that was

that. Do you know, I think if I had claimed that they were duelling scars, she would have believed me. For all her generation know, everyone over the age of thirty strolled down the ramp of Noah's Ark on the first nice morning after the Flood. Our early lives are, to them, snippets of Ancient History. More students these days than I care to contemplate have difficulty in distinguishing between two world wars. Generally, I find such glimpses into their chasms of ignorance dispiriting; but on this occasion her sheer benightedness filled me with something akin to relief. The barriers between us strengthened again, and after a moment I felt free to ask, 'Do they still worry you?'

'What?'

'These scars. These scars on my face. Do they worry you?'

'They're *hideous*. Really *hideous*.'

Out, just like that. Out in the open between us. And finding I had no reply to make, I took refuge in a bout of fine chopping. You wait a lifetime for someone to come straight out with it – Margaret never said anything remotely like that in sixteen years – and when, at last, it happens, you find you've lost, no, never even learned, the way to answer candour with candour. Did she even notice how disconcerted I was by her outburst? I don't believe she did. She simply transferred her attention from the chopped celery to the small pile of rinsed lettuce in front of her, picking out the freshest leaves and shredding them, stuffing the pieces into her mouth and talking through them. Floodgates had opened, clearly. She was chatting away, totally at ease.

'It is an awful pity, your getting those scars. Without them you might have been a fairly reasonable-looking man. The other side of your face almost looks nice, from the back.'

She looked up at me. Can it possibly have been for my approval? Lord knows if she truly believed I might be grateful for this worse than back-handed compliment. All I know is, she took my warning look for mere rebuttal, and carried on.

'No, it is, really. If you sit right at the side of the seminar room, by the door—'

'Like you do?'

This cold interjection she took for simple statement of fact, and went on regardless.

'Like I do, yes, you can see hardly any scarring at all. You look almost all right. And if you let your hair grow a bit longer, you'd look even more normal. It's rather odd, I must say, the way you look so different, depending on which side shows. Everyone does, of course. Not quite so much as you, naturally. But everyone has a good and a bad side. I know I do. This side's all right' – her hand, on its way over to the lettuce, sidetracked to touch her lovely face – 'but I think I'm really ugly from the other. Really ugly.'

I don't believe I've ever heard anything so foolish. Almost without thinking, I brought the chopping-knife down, hard, on the very leaf for which she was reaching. Anyone else would have been startled into looking up and seeing just how angry I had become. There wasn't any missing the tone of my voice now.

'You'll possibly appreciate that someone as disfigured

41

as I am finds other people's notions of good and bad profiles distinctly absurd!'

Incredibly, she was already trying to prise the lettuce out from beneath the still shuddering knife blade. I might just as well not have bothered to speak. Clearly, to get Alicia Davie's attention, I'd have to go ahead and chop her fingers off. And I was still staring at her in astonishment when she looked up and smiled with just the smallest hint of coquetry.

'Can I have more of that nice wine?'

That's it, I remember thinking, as she slid her glass over the table towards me. That's it! I was delivered at last into a modicum of enlightenment. Neither I nor my anger existed for Alicia. We were not real. And that apparent and most beguiling openness of hers, the all-too-quick human responses, even her knack for saying things others never would or could, the things that so mercilessly assailed and touched, all these were the result. They gave the illusion of intimacy; but an illusion was all it was. Indeed, it was illusion created with all the more ease simply because at root there was so little there, such tenuous contact, so limited an awareness. I brought a knife blade down a hair's breadth from her fingertips, and her friendly unfeeling prattle had never so much as faltered. She didn't, I realized with a bit of a shudder, inhabit the same world as I do and you do, where other people's feelings show and matter. Don't think I don't know what I'm talking about. I've taught for years. A lot of young people have passed through my hands and many of them have been inward or shy, gauche or unsure. I recognize these characteristics in most of their disguises, and I'm used to them. They don't overly concern me. I can distinguish them from their more serious counterparts, the traits exhibited by those who wander in and out of classes ringed by some ghastly modern equivalent of thorny hedges, their isolation almost entire, their links with other people little more than mirage. I might not be 'chatty' with students, but I pay attention. Often I am the first to recognize those small tell-tale signs of disintegration, the widening fissures of personality when that protective shell over self begins to crack and peel away. I'm rarely taken by surprise by any of the names I see on those small white slips from the Health Centre that surface in my in-tray from time to time, announcing the official hiatus in some young person's academic life.

But this, this was different. This was something else entirely. A kind of personal imprisonment I hadn't seen before and wouldn't expect to find in such a girl – clever, pretty, getting along passably well with her work, no obvious problems. What was it? Something not right, or why should I feel as if, for her, I wasn't even standing there? Letting the knife drop, I leaned my weight upon the table top and gave Miss Davie a good long look. While she munched lettuce, I had my moment of insight. Could this, I thought, be nothing more or less than simple, crass insensitivity? Could it? And even now, all these months later, all I can tell you is that nothing that happened afterwards ever convinced me that it was not.

She slid her empty glass closer towards me.

'Can I?'

I pulled myself together.

'Alicia, you can have anything I have to offer you.'

43

And I meant it.

It was a good meal in every way, I made quite sure of that. I led her through it, handling her with that precision born of understanding and confidence, tempting her with warm, good-tasting food and quiet attention to feel entirely at her ease in my house and my company. Difference in age is the most significant of inequalities. Maturity, with its henchmen, patience and experience, gives control. I controlled her. I had no gains in mind, no hidden motive. Indeed, I thought I already had what I wanted. She'd come, and had not borne the most casual inspection. I had unearthed deficiencies in her sufficient to purge obsession at a stroke. A free man once again, I laid my offerings on the plates and set them down in front of her, deriving pleasure from her pleasure and happy, more than happy, simply to feed her and listen, glad that she talked, no matter what nonsense it was she was saying. She ate and chattered and chattered and ate. Her cheeks flushed and, as time passed, her gawky tenseness loosened to a level of physical ease that I confess to having found a shade disconcerting at my own table. Wine made her amusing. She told me a joke or two, reeled off with some wit and far more invention a stream of scandal about my colleagues, described a disastrous student rally, criticized in the most minute particulars the organization of my department. She accepted without demur a second, and then a third, cup of coffee, ignored my increasingly frequent glances at the sweeping hand of the wall-clock, and, when I rose, stiff-kneed, and went into the bedroom to seek out a book to prove a small point, followed me through.

It is important, how it happened. To me it matters, now you know the end, that you should understand the beginning. I'm not a man for telling lies, or spreading his own self-serving gloss upon the way things were. All that I tell you is the truth. This is what happened.

She worked her way around the room, around to me. There's little more to it than that. Beginning with the photographs upon the mantelpiece, she set upon me. Who's this? Who's Margaret? She didn't know that I was married. Well, if I was divorced, had Margaret married again? How soon? Who to? Who's this, then? My grandmother? Was she dead yet? What a vile vase – did I *win* it? She liked the writing-desk, though. Very old. And did my grandmother leave me that lovely mirror, too? It was hanging too far up the wall, it should be moved down, not everybody was that tall. And who was this on the bookcase? My *mother*? She didn't look a bit like me!

'Ah, but as you yourself have pointed out, I come from the hideous side of the family.'

An embarrassed pause, a guilty giggle, and – would you believe it? – she was off again. Nice rug, nice colour. Did – what-was-her-name? Margaret? – make that huge macramé lampshade? Why didn't she take it with her when she left? She would have.

I sank down on the end of my bed, weak partly from the effort of making my first joke ever at the expense of my unprepossessing countenance, partly from sheer fright at watching her prowl and finger and pry into my most private things.

Socks and stuff in here, right? That door's a cupboard,

yes? She'd never seen me wear that jacket, or those heavy walking shoes. A double bed, and just for me? And a real feather duvet! Were they as wonderful to sleep under as everyone said?

'You should give it a try.'

She turned.

'With you?'

'Alicia, I'm old enough to be your father!'

'So?'

Oh, the coolness, almost insolence, of it. And the ease with which she settled beside me. I swear that it was she who touched me first, putting out her hand and laying it flat upon the ruts and botches of my face as if the mere trace of a touch of hers could turn the ravages as smooth as butter.

'Come on, then.'

'Alicia, please. Go home now.'

I tried. I tried.

Did we have intercourse on that occasion? I wouldn't call what we had intercourse. I'd call it rape. I sat there, paralysed with horror, a latter-day Richard III watching the endless line of grisly apparitions materialize and threaten – the Dean, the Principal, her parents, my colleagues. Even my mother and grandmother gazed down in shocked reproof from their framed squares while she unwrapped me, unpeeled me like an unresisting and insentient banana – tie, shirt, shoes, socks, everything – all the time rubbing, licking, stroking, provoking. She pushed me back onto the bed, and I had neither strength nor strength of mind to stop her. She set about unmanning me until there was no going back. A man can't suddenly call Pax, or Last Bus, or Wrong Time of the Month, can he? I'd had no woman in my bed since Margaret left it. Urgency took up where common sense left off. Yes, we had intercourse on that occasion. Yes.

Chapter 3

I didn't know I had a body till I met her. Does that sound silly? Listen, some days I walk into that amphitheatre over there to lecture, and look around at all of them, leaning against one another's shoulders, wearing one another's clothes as often as not, companionably tucking their neighbour's feet under their woollies as soon as the heating system breaks down, and I tell myself firmly: all this is easily explained away. It's youth, that's all. They're fresh from school. The easy and unfettered physical closeness of all those rolling, communal playpens has not yet had time to become abraded. People my age used to be young, must have been easy, squeeze-as-you-please once, too.

It isn't true, though. Oh, you know. You're not so far in age from me that you have no inkling of what I'm talking about. Don't think the reason you sit listening so patiently hasn't occurred to me. It's not your way, now that you're older, now that you've reached a comfortable rung on your particular career ladder, as I have on mine, to settle simply for knowing what happened, like any callow junior officer bent single-mindedly on speedy promotion. No, you'd like to understand, though understanding takes more time. And you're prepared to spend time more freely now that, like me, you have so much less of it left to spend. It isn't only time, either, is it? You know as well as I do that it's not just me we're learning about here today.

You know what I am trying to get at. It makes a difference, coming into the world with one of these raw, modern birth dates. These students aren't just younger versions of their grandmothers. They're a new species entirely, reared, after revolution, by revolutionaries. They must be different, touching men's bodies as they do, oblivious to that terror of physical and spiritual consequences which paralysed so many of their grannies. Me, I've no standards of comparison. I know next to nothing. I was a virgin till I slept with my wife. But you, you must have been a fair-looking laddie. Think back. You may have had a willing girl in your bed before you married and settled down, but could you sleep with her? I mean, could you *sleep*? Could *she* sleep, haunted by the common spectres: had she glanced at the wrong month of the calendar? Was the small, sore place deep within her the result of passion overly prolonged, or the first telltale sign of ineradicable disease? And would you bother to cross the street when you caught sight of her the next morning? She'd been told often enough, I'm sure, that a man doesn't run after a bus once he's caught it. She might feel pleasure, but not sleep soundly after it. And if she couldn't sleep, then how could you, crushed hard against the wall by all those extra bedfellows of hers: Guilt and Anxiety and Fear?

Things really aren't like that any longer. You and I hear the moralists drone on, 'sensing a new mood', 'seeing the pendulum begin to swing the other way', 'expecting the backlash'; but so far as I can make out, the ones they're talking at aren't even listening. They're too busy sleeping together, first in the one sense and then in the other, deeply and well. You can, I'm told, barge in on them in the morning, and all they do is burrow farther down together under the bedding, groaning, just like any old married couple. Nobody tells them what to do with their bodies any more – not God, not Mum and Dad, the landlady or the Dean of Arts. The only one to whom they lend an ear is that friendly doctor down at the family planning clinic. They own their bodies, and it makes a difference. If all the women you knew had owned theirs all those years ago, surely your life would have run down some very different pathways. Surely you, too, would be different now.

Not me, of course. I can at least take consolation in the fact that no sexual sea-change coming a decade or two earlier would have had any impact on me. Nobody fancied me, and when you've got a face like mine you don't go round making advances. As young as seven, I knew that. Invited to a birthday party, I'd stand aside for 'Spin the Bottle' and 'Postman's Knock', and though some mother, noticing me through the kitchen doorway, might take a moment to ruffle my hair or chat to me kindly, she'd never come up with the Open Sesame: 'Let Ian in, now.' Youth I remember as a purgatory of futile sentiment nourished by endlessly frustrated flesh. On my twenty-first birthday my father gave me fifty pounds, and I immediately thought of purchasing a woman's favours, just for one night. But I'd been raised sufficiently principled to recognize that it wouldn't be fair on the victim. So I kissed no-one before Margaret, and I'm still in the dark about what must have suddenly swept over me that I should just that once have circumnavigated the vicious reefs of physical embarrassment, screwed myself up sufficiently to lean across and, taking her entirely by surprise, lay my twisted mouth firmly on hers.

She didn't care much for my kissing her, that I could tell; and over the years we lived together I pressed this form of affection on her less and less. I came to see she'd never really get to like it; and I grew fonder of her as time passed, came to appreciate all her good qualities. The notion of subjecting such a nice person to something she didn't really care for at all became to me less and less attractive.

But she didn't object to my body. Indeed, I believe she quite liked it. More often than you might imagine, it was Margaret who reached out for me between the sheets, though, once I had begun to respond with quickening interest to her initiatory caresses, she would lapse promptly back into recipient passivity. I mustn't stop, no. But I must go on in a way that suited her, and what suited Margaret was the undistracting dark, impersonal silence and, on my part, a kind of delicate and finely tuned persistence, a knack of touching her as seemingly impossible to master at the start as letting in the clutch on a car; once learned, just as straightforward and, one might add a little churlishly, just as matter-of-course. By the time I was sanctioned by her small shudder of release to slide into a higher gear concordant with my own pattern of need, I was as often as not already thinking about something else. Looking back, I am inclined to believe that Margaret and I got on together in bed no worse than many other long-married couples, better than some. But there was nothing happening on our firm, well-chosen, orthopaedic mattress to prompt her to reconsider her decision, once it was made, to leave me, or, for that matter, to encourage me to beg her to stay.

I find it curious, this dampening effect that she and I had on one another. It's not what I would have expected at all. As far back as I can remember, sex to me seemed the most exciting, most dangerous and delicious of pastimes. I must have wasted half my early life daydreaming, yearning, ready to sell my soul for one small chance at what I suspected almost every adult and half my peers of doing most of the hours they were out of my sight – lovemaking. I saw my disfigurement as the only barrier between my sexual isolation and wanton coupling. It loomed so large it overshadowed all other potential obstacles to the extent of rendering them invisible to me. And I assumed that everyone else, though they might tactfully keep it from me, was forever doing what I sincerely believed I'd be doing too if only I had been permitted to keep that halfway-to-passable face which grinned out from the faded photographs well hidden away in my mother's dresser. My bodily state was one of continual ferment and turmoil. I was convinced that, if ever I were blessed with a woman (and, as you might guess, fantasies of beautiful but helpless blind virgins played their part here), I would spend all the hours God sends in bed with her, making up for lost time. In fact, I married in the spring of 1956, and, by September, was spending evenings and weekends lining the four walls of my study with fitted bookshelves. Margaret would wander in and out, passing the odd companionable remark, the gimlet, or a fresh cup of tea. I was, by twenty-five, a sexually disappointed man, and yet it didn't seem all that important.

And what of Margaret? I wonder, did I ever give to her the pleasure that she failed to give me? I'm forced to answer that I very much doubt it. Pleasure, I know now, runs through the body like fire-water, lifting the spirits, touching the soul. That kind of incandescence can't be hidden any more than it can be feigned. All I gave Margaret was satisfaction, and she seemed satisfied with that. She did, after all, stay with me sixteen years, paid me the consolatory and face-saving compliment of only leaving when she met another man who suited her better. Alasdair Mackie's wife moved out into a cold and lonely bed-sitter. I can't have been half as awful to live with as Mackie. But clearly I was no great shakes either, and great shakes is what you'll toss the world away for when you're young and when you're old. The wonder is that time between, that stark emotional midwinter bondage to other things – the house, the burgeoning career, the education of the children. Weighing like sodden earth upon a coffin, these things can keep the love of pleasure buried for twenty years, but not for ever. Even my Margaret suddenly felt impelled to reach through the prison grey of married life towards a shaft of outside sunlight that seemed to her to blaze the way to release. Even she threw off the shackles of drab security we'd forged around ourselves, and went for something brighter and richer. (Certainly he's richer. I wouldn't say he's any brighter.)

Leaving me. And, by the very act of leaving, reawakening in me that old, old sense of something missed, of never having had even a glimpse of something, somewhere, out there on offer. I am an equable man. I can wait years for things to come along to me, and brook it if they never do. Nevertheless, when gifts are rare, a man can't be expected to turn them down. I lost the battle for strength like that decades ago when, in that growling, mauling flurry by the garden wall, I was made irretrievably ugly, and, though I wasn't to realize it for years, offers like Alicia Davie's teasing 'With you?' became, to me, infinitely precious.

I tried, though. I tried.

'Alicia, I'm old enough to be your father!'

'So?'

She was right, too. What the hell was the matter with that? There's nothing much wrong with my body. It's heavier than it used to be, perhaps a bit slower, body hair greying. It's none the worse for any of that. I wasn't going to traumatize or damage her, and even if one still believed virginity to be, in some sense, important, she'd no virginity to lose. She wasn't going to be disgraced, or undone, or bring some unwanted baby into the world. I

55

hadn't even used the powers of my age and position to bolster her seduction into anything more serious than eating my food and drinking my coffee. Going up this fresh avenue of experience was her idea. Remember, this was a baby of the revolution. I told you, they think differently: nice meal, feel good, what shall we both do now?

'Come on, then.'

It was in my defence more than in hers that I ran up my last, weakly fluttering flag of resistance.

'Alicia, please. Go home now.'

Did she even hear me? I don't believe she did, so busy was she with the laces, the buckle, the knot, the buttons, all of the things that keep a man safe.

'God, all this stuff all over you. How can you stand it?'

I swatted feebly at her as my shoes were pushed, one after the other, over the edge of the bed. The great unneighbourly clonks they made in falling conjured a vision of Miss Ballantyne beneath, turning towards her ceiling a face suffused with disapproval indistinguishable from that of my framed forebears on the mantelpiece.

'Alicia, stop it.'

'Stop what? Oh, sorry'

Great God, she thought I wanted her to stop pulling off my rather good shirt without first undoing every button.

'No, not that. Stop it. Stop what you're doing.'

'Stop, stop,' she mimicked in a faint, high voice. 'Oh, stop. You mustn't touch me. Stop, stop, stop.' The zip slid down under persistent tugging, her hand slipped in, and with a swift, experienced wriggle manoeuvred around the very last of my old-fashioned bastions of protection.

'Y-fronts!'

'For God's sake!'

'Are they?'

'Alicia!'

'They are! White Y-fronts. Just like my dad's!'

There's nothing like the mention of a girl's father to haul a man back to his senses. I jack-knifed upright with an adroitness and strength of purpose for which anyone watching a moment before would not have given me credit. Catching her wrists, I shouted at her, 'Now pack it in, or I shall slap you!'

Astonishment. And then a shiver of excitement, quite unmistakable, a thin and unequivocal runnel of real arousal broke through her facile barrage of sexual artifice, shutting her up and stilling her assault. I felt the calmer for seeing it. This first, small, transient indication of her real feelings reminded me of what I still firmly believed were mine; and, holding her wrists down firmly for safety's sake, I opened up between us on the bed my professional portfolio, prepared to rustle the contents gently at her: This Won't Do; You Must Go Home Now; I Have a Special Responsibility, both as a Teacher and as Head of Department, for your Tranquillity and Protection. And there was plenty more where that lot came from. In getting on for thirty years of teaching, I've seen enough to know relationships of this complexion almost invariably end in distress and bitterness and, all too often, allegations of unethical professional conduct.

'Alicia, my sweet. Look at this mess,' I started in all good faith. But she looked up. She lifted up her face and looked. Quite mistaking my figurative meaning, she shook back her hair, raised her head, looked me in the face – all of it; not just the calm, still, grey no-man's-land of my undamaged eyes, but all the rest of it as well, the mess she thought I was referring to, the scar patch. She took her time, and was honest about it, flinching a little with revulsion at the very worst scallops, dwelling on certain confusing corrugations as if an explanation for each particular ingrown twist of flesh was there somehow to be deciphered. It wasn't what I'd meant when I said 'Look at this mess'; but once she began, I couldn't for the world have stopped her. No-one has ever looked at me before, you understand, bar those protected from the horror of the sight by the immunity of white coats and professional interest. I had to let her. I had to know if she could do it. I even let go of her wrists. I watched her looking, and reckoned it to be as new and awkward an experience for me as for her. I felt far more vulnerable than when she'd slipped her hand inside my trousers. I rank myself along with the deformed in that the words 'private places' mean something very different to me than to you.

I waited. She kept on looking. Then she put out a hand to push the half-unbuttoned shirt back off my shoulder. It slid down my back, impeding my arms, but I didn't move to disturb her. She'd left her hand exactly where the shirt had lain against my neck, here, under my collar, where the worst of it, the deepest runnel, goes. She stuck her finger in the ditch of it, and ran her finger down to the very end where I become, like everybody else, a smooth skin plain; and then she ran it back again, right up, past where she started, back up into the damage of my face, choosing any old path around the lumps, through whorls and corrugations, playing at mazes with it, only touching, but, by touch alone, stinging the inexperienced skin into a fresh, tear-springing reminder of that first hard slap of the side of her hand across the same few inches of scarring. Everything I planned to say to her burned up, forgotten, in the face of more important things.

'See? *See?* Look at it. *Look* at it. See how it is? I'm *different*. I'm not like anything you've ever come across before. And I'm not up for any little games of sexual favours, eyes tightly closed, safe in the dark. I've *had* all that, and I don't want it any more. I'm finished with graciously averted eyes. and I'm not interested in kindly physical charity!' I took her wrists again, and shook her hard. 'Understand this, little Alicia. I'm *done* with sympathy and generosity and all half measures. To get to me, you have to go in through the scar patch here. There isn't any other way!' I shook her harder, till she gasped. 'That's right. Think! Think about it! *Think!*'

The skin of her wrists paled round my tightening thumbs. Who's to say if another's thinking? What goes on in a head is quite unfathomable. I watched the shape of her eyes appear to change under the barrage of my hostility and felt her pulses quicken in the grip of my fingers, but I had no way of knowing what she thought, or if she thought at all, before she whispered through rising tears, 'You're *hurting* me.'

'I *mean* to.'

'Stop it!'

'And will you promise me that you will go?'

59

Silence. And then the smallest shake of the head. A very quiet, almost inaudible, 'No.'

Well, there it is. You bring them up with equal rights, they get so that they, too, won't take no for an answer. And that was it so far as I was concerned. I was beaten. I'd done my best, warned her, threatened and frightened her and bruised her little wrists. What more can a man do? I'd fought an exhausting passion for her for weeks. I had no energy left to fight her.

Surrendering, I lay back on the bed.

'Well, then. Get on with it.'

Get on with it she certainly did. To my mind, there's not been anything to match it for sheer and glorious physical expertise since Brown's eldest whirled round and round the narrow parapet of the Union Building upon her skateboard, waving the banner *Rectify the Anomaly*. Small wonder so many of today's students can't write a grammatical sentence. Such awesome proficiency in these other skills must take its toll of time and energy, and leave them weaker in wits. You'd think the whole of her was fingertips, the way she went on. There didn't seem one inch of herself she didn't use to quarry pleasure out of me, or one inch of myself she left unscathed by mouth and hands and all the hillocks and hollows of her sweet body. She had no sense of personal trespass, none at all. Margaret would never in all our sixteen years of sharing a bed have dreamed of touching me in ways and places Alicia took for granted. She moved so I hardly knew where she was from one moment to the next, and yet it was she who kept surfacing to whisper fiercely in my ear, 'Keep *still*,' until she'd hurt me, shocked me, worn me down and out, made me so sore and given me one last blinding shaft of pleasure so overwhelming that I obeyed.

After, in peace and quiet, I prodded her from sleep to demand through the tangled hedge of her hair, 'Where did you learn all that, then?'

She wriggled. That warm, damp skin rubbed easily against mine. Her mouth hard up against my shoulder, I could scarcely make out the mocking reply.

'Passiondale.

It made its own sense. I hadn't for a moment believed she'd picked all that lot up somewhere like Peebles.

Chapter 4

She was no prisoner, and I want to make that clear at the outset. There was no question of my holding her, cajoling or intimidating her to stay. Quite the reverse. On that first morning I intimated my own attitude towards the possibility of a continuing relationship with neither pressure nor blandishments. Indeed, I was little short of curt. I rose early, washed and shaved in privacy, then pottered about my kitchen listening to the radio's account of the previous day's parliamentary proceedings, setting out matching breakfast plates, tipping a little marmalade from the jar into a small cut-glass bowl, evenly toasting the slices of bread and cutting them in half diagonally. I was, I admit, uncomfortably aware that to anyone accustomed to the comprehensive squalor of 18A, Ardmory Road, these small appurtenances of civilized life might double as snares; but since it was unclear

63

to me how, short of my tipping the poor child out on to the streets unfed, their use could be eschewed, I carried on and set the table as I always do, except that, for the first time since Margaret left me, I set for two.

At half past eight I went back into the bedroom. I looked down at her in my bed, still fast asleep, and my heart turned over. 'If you were to get up now,' I told her, 'we could breakfast together before I'm forced to leave.' She opened her eyes in time to see me laying my dressing-gown on the bed beside her. Back in the kitchen I sat at the table and held my head in my hands – a posture into which I found myself slipping disturbingly often – and was relieved when she came in, breaking a most disquieting train of thought.

Our breakfast together was a quiet occasion. I made a point of saying little for fear of saying very much more. Alicia appeared still to be asleep; that, or the carefully laid table, cocoon of a home around her dishevelled morning self, brought out in her the frank and unbuttered manners of childhood: a steady, uncommunicative munching, unconscious scratchings of the tangled hair, silent stretchings across the table for items more politely asked for and passed.

Once she said, looking over at my plate, 'That's clever.'
'What?'
'That. What you're doing.'
I looked down at the triangles of toast that lay together on my plate. My knife paused in the act of spreading butter across both halves of the square.
'What?'
'Buttering both pieces at once. That's very clever.'

I was appalled, simply appalled.

'It is', I said, 'the sort of thing a chimpanzee could work out for itself.'

She shrugged. Clearly, for all that, she still thought it clever. I wanted to shout at her across the table, 'Alicia! For God's sake kiss me, or I shall throw the toast-rack at you!' Instead, I scraped my chair back and left the room as casually as if I'd just heard the morning paper fall with a slap on the doormat. When I returned, hatted, scarved and briefcased, she was still swallowing tea, finishing up toast. I checked her expression of surprise by coming out directly with the short speech I'd composed whilst shaving, the brief announcement into which I'd put so much thought. If it seems overly terse, bear in mind that the principal consideration was to avoid undue pressure.

I said to her, 'There is a doorkey under the rim of your plate, in case you should choose to return and I am not here.'

I was out of the door and down the stone staircase before she could even have taken in the gist of this, let alone started coming to terms with all its subtle, open-ended edges. Reaching the street, I realized that I had left my spectacles folded beside the toast-rack, but there was no going back. I strode off towards the university, the skin of the unblemished side of my face as highly coloured as the other, my thoughts and senses, like my vision, blurred. The entire morning was a misery. Mishandling through sheer distraction a meeting in which I took the chair, I failed to manage to steer through a couple of matters that I considered critical for the future smooth running of the department. In the wake of my irritation at this result, I allowed another of my colleagues, a man I regard as working at the boundaries of his competence, to outmanoeuvre me on the important issue of teaching loads. My eleven o'clock lecture fell flat. I returned from the amphitheatre to find my spectacles lying on the secretary's desk, but no note, no message, no hint. It was a worse than wasted day. I would have done better to have spent the hours in bed, except that just the passing thought of my bed now deranged me. I wouldn't care to admit to you how slowly each hour passed.

At four o'clock there came a barely audible scratching on the wooden panels of my door, and I knew who it was even before I heard her say, 'Am I disturbing you?'

'Not at all,' I told her. 'I welcome breaks.'

This is the end of the line, I thought; and thank God for it.

'Look—'

'Please shut the door, Alicia.'

She pushed the door closed, and flattened herself against it, as though keeping as far as possible from an untrustworthy animal.

'Well?'

'Look—'

'My name's not Look. It's Ian.'

She was silent. I realized with some astonishment that I had floored her. She couldn't, in spite of all that had happened between us the night before, call me by name.

'Alicia?'

'It's a bit difficult.'

'Difficult?'

She scoured the room, the ceiling, walls and book-shelves for help.

'It's about Brightmony . . .'

'Ah.'

So. She'd come to tell me she had, at the last moment, decided to go home to Brightmony for the weekend. It was a tactful and becoming form of rejection, and a small, untouched part of me was pleased that she had thought of it.

'You don't mind?'

'Alicia, it is no longer a matter of minding. There was a time for minding once, but I'm way past that now.'

'So you don't mind?'

How cruel and selfish the young are, I thought, to want you not to mind when they twist their long knives.

'No. I don't mind.'

'So I can bring him?'

'Who?'

'*Brightmony*. Can I *bring* him? I can't leave him alone another whole day. I promise he won't scratch the furni-ture.'

My head went back into my hands. 'Yes, yes. Yes, you may bring your cat, Alicia.'

There is, as we both know, no fool like an old fool.

The promise of a cat lover is worth nothing. Before the weekend was out, my chair-backs were in shreds, my sofa ruined, a strange stain had materialized on the floor of the bathroom and, on the Monday morning, from heaps of cooling ashes within the living-room grate, a most sus-picious smell emanated. I made a particular point of not investigating, and left the flat in a hurry. I found on my return, laden with groceries, that though Alicia had gone to the trouble of hauling the heavy chairs farther against the wall to try to hide the evidence of the worst ravages of Brightmony's claws on their loose covers, the smell still lingered. Sighing, I dropped to my knees and reached for the little brass shovel.

Those next few weeks, they take some explanation. I've thought about it over and over. I began thinking then, in those moments in front of the grate, and I reverted to it as a topic of reflection time and again. Why ever did she come back, day after day? Why ever did I let her? Clearly, in one all too obvious sense, I wanted her. Desires and actions, however, are worlds apart, and men like me have every reason on earth for keeping them so – job, reputation, conscience, even self-esteem. Alicia Davie was hardly what you might call 'my type'. Quite the reverse. She was a messy and an indolent girl and, as I came to suspect when the telephone bill came in, deceitful too. She ate continually between meals, a habit I despise and abhor. The clothes she wore were almost wholly repellent. A number of students manage to give style to garments more commonly found abandoned on park benches than hanging in wardrobes, but she looked, frankly, like walking jumble. And notwithstanding her own weakness in the sartorial sphere, I found her needlessly offensive about my own manner of dress, and in particular my rather old-fashioned style of underwear. Indeed, she was little short of rude on occasions. Worse, she was deeply, deeply ignorant. Sometimes I'd wonder how a man like me could possibly be sharing a breakfast table, a bathroom, a bed with someone like her. It reminded me more than anything of National Service, the only other period of my life when every possession, however personal, was suddenly assumed to be communal, every silence was religiously broken, and every single activity, however commonplace, however tedious, had to be undertaken to the constant accompaniment of witless commentary. She'd watch me rise and dress. I'd see her grave eyes following me about the room, and wonder what on earth she was thinking. Then she'd come out with it.

'Ian, I reckon you must clean your shoes every morning.'

It is a fact. I always have.

'"A solitary life cherishes mere fancies until they become manias."'

'Who says?'

'Mrs Gaskell.'

'Is she your cleaning lady?'

Believe me, that small exchange is not at all untypical of the sort of intercourse to which Alicia and I were reduced out of the bed. But I found her soothing, liberating, utterly cheering. The thought of pleasure banished all anxiety in her and, by extension, in me. I lost touch entirely with my responsibilities when I was with her. Once I looked up from marking my way through a heap of essays on the role of pressure groups within the British political system, and asked her, 'Alicia, why did you choose to study political science?' There was a long pause, and then she answered, 'I don't know.' I waited, but after a bit it seemed clear that nothing more was forthcoming, and soon she drifted off to watch the television. 'I don't know.' What sort of answer is that to a Professor of Politics? She'd evidently quite forgotten I was one. And more and more often, catching sight of her body in doorways and mirrors and pale reflections from the window panes, I could forget I was too.

Only at home, though. I never took her out. I kept her well hidden. I promptly discontinued my custom of extending hospitality to visiting speakers, colleagues or students. 'Workmen,' I claimed, as I'd heard others claiming 'kitchen renovation' or 'dry rot' to immediate effect. I would leave at ferociously early hours in the mornings, and make sure our times of return never coincided. 'Will you be able to walk home with me around four?' I'd ask her on the days I knew Brown would keep her until five-thirty. On other days I'd claim I'd no idea what time this meeting, that discussion group, or some pre-arranged transatlantic telephone call would be finished. I was, to be honest, embarrassed about being seen with her in public. We ate at home. I tried to put it to myself that this was simply because I like to cook, and especially enjoyed cooking for her, feeding her just what she felt like eating precisely when she felt like eating it, without the bother of our walking out and walking back, and finishing up as much as we could of what I paid for. But there was more to it than that. I was ashamed, both of her and of myself. The closest it came to disturbing me was one day when, passing her with an unobtrusive wink in the departmental corridor, I found myself turning to Brown on an impulse, and asking, 'What do you think of Davie?'

'Who?'

'Davie. Alicia Davie. The one who just passed us.'

'She's all right. Why?'

I didn't respond, and, within a moment or two, he had forgotten I had asked him a question, let alone what it was. But I was left with the uneasy feeling of having sailed too near the wind professionally, of the crucial importance of keeping these two halves of my life strictly and totally apart. Guilt and self-disgust, dogs tamed and closeted at home, snarled with a disconcerting fierceness whilst out walking.

In very many ways, though, Alicia and I got on well. She was affectionate and easy-going. She was soft-spoken, with long quiet patches. Indeed, it more than once occurred to me that from time to time she used drugs. Some evenings, when I came back from work, she wasn't in the flat. She'd slip in later, a little furtively; and if I let drop that I'd wondered about her whereabouts, she'd mutter something practically inaudible along the lines of having gone to 'pick up a few things from Ardmory Road'. There never were any 'things' though; and on these evenings she had an aura of reverie about her that struck me as owing as much to chemical fine adjustments within her brain as to meditative inclinations within her nature. Did I ask her if she took drugs? No, I did not. I'm not in the habit of asking people about their private lives. I attach some value to my own privacy, and I treat others accordingly. I'm not, as Americans say, 'into sharing'. I think the world would turn into a bear-garden if everyone went round asking their friends and acquaintances for information those very people could, if they chose, vouchsafe entirely of their own accord. Though I don't want by this to suggest that we didn't ever discuss things. Alicia had a way of raising quite intimate matters: not putting my back up by asking me outright what I was doing or thinking or feeling; rather by coming out with her impressions of my state of mind or body. She left me, as it were, free to correct or expand on her intuitions, or not, as I chose. She'd say things like 'You look as though you've been through the wringer,' and I would find myself describing to her in some small detail a trying meeting of the Budget Committee. Or 'Your body's all stiff tonight,' she'd tell me. And not wanting her to mis-understand, I'd find myself explaining my occasional physical withdrawals in ways I never could with Margaret. Alicia never asked, you see. She never demanded or nagged or persisted. Women are all too often raised to think of themselves as born with a gift for intimacy. A man like me more often thinks of them as harpies. Alicia wasn't like that. She let me be. She even let my sporadic bouts of tetchiness float over her head, never causing their escalation into full-blooded ill temper, as Margaret used to, by making seemingly endless concerned enquiries as to the cause. In any event, irritability in a man my age is very often born of simple fatigue. Alicia pleased me by taking to my habit of napping on weekend after-noons as naturally as a duck takes to water. She had here, it has to be admitted, the head start of being by nature bone idle. I minded this indolence of hers, and, there again, I didn't mind it. I'd mind the breakfast dishes wallowing, still unrinsed, in the kitchen sink when I came home after a long and tedious day of frustrating phone calls and being civil to visiting speakers. I'd walk in and mind the mess, the cat hairs, the heaps of dropped clothes, the tell-tale trails of biscuit crumbs across the floors to litter nests of her indifferently thought out, half-written essays. I'd mind the grubby thumb prints on my good reference books, the newspaper that looked, daily, more as though she had knitted with it than read it. I'd mind the lights left burning, the rumpled bed, the bottles of milk left souring on top of the refrigerator, the smears of butter on my dressing-gown sleeves. I'd walk into the bathroom, girded to upbraid her, and after one look at that pink-flushed perfect skin, the soft soaking tendrils of damp hair around her ears, the small round islands of her knees in the water, I didn't mind again. If you don't love a woman when she's sitting in your bath, then you don't love her.

Was she in love with me? No. No, she wasn't. She only loved that bloody cat. He was the only creature in the world for whom she seemed to have any real feeling. On any day she'd know how long he'd slept, whether he'd dreamed, how much he'd eaten, what he'd been doing with himself. She knew his moods, his needs, his likes and dislikes down to his favourite caresses. She'd even stir herself sufficiently to traipse out in cold or wet or dark to buy him milk and cat food. He was the fond recipient of anything unselfish I saw in her, all true affection. Over the years she'd clearly squeezed him and rubbed him and cried into his fur and carried him about until he had become a part of her. She loved that cat in ways she'd never love a human being. She knew his birth date (never asked me mine), read out his horoscope before her own, and wouldn't dream of offering him the same canned

73

flavour of cat food twice in a row. Sometimes I'd watch her lying on her stomach on a rug, apparently absorbed in some loud and cheap television show, and suddenly her hand would stretch out behind her, her little fingers wriggling with welcome, her whole body entirely receptive. I'd wonder, for a moment, if she were reaching out for me. But there was something in the ease and warmth of the gesture that led me to doubt it. I'd glance behind my chair and, sure enough, a moment later Brightmony would silently materialize in the doorway. There's nothing weak about my hearing. She hadn't heard him coming. She simply knew.

A pity she wasn't as sensitive with me. I bought her flowers and she let them die for want of water and a jug. She shunted the little treats I cooked around her plate indifferently. She lost the silver wristwatch I gave her for her birthday within a week. And, giggling over some infelicity of style, she spilled coffee on the only copy I still possess of my first book. I seemed to count for nothing. Listen, one day, rooting around my desk and drawers and filing-cabinets, she came across my lecture notes for Comparative Government II. Now I've taught this course, and courses like it, on and off for years. I have a well-kept basic set of typewritten notes. I may, in lecturing, add an example or two from recent political practice, or develop more fully a topic of particular current interest to me or certain of my audience. But basically I give the same course every year I teach it. Once she discovered these notes, Alicia Davie never again bothered to attend any of my lectures. She read the notes and stayed at home in bed instead. Is that the behaviour of a woman in love? You know as well as I do it's not. But me, I was in love. I was a fool for it, standing up there on the podium delivering my weighty, well-worn gems of knowledge, half out of my mind from missing, somewhere in the sea of bland, bored faces in front of me, hers.

She did continue to attend my seminars, though; and in the face of Warner, MacFaddyen, McKinley and, on the increasingly rare occasions on which he favoured us with his presence, Scott-Watson, I was discreet. Once, only once, I let slip the mask of pedagogical detachment. Provoked beyond prudence by her tonsil-baring indications of boredom during a brief excursion into Mill's attitude towards political participation, I said to her with more than a little menace, 'Keep up the heavy yawning, Alicia, and you'll find yourself on the floor.'

Her mouth clamped shut and stayed that way for the remaining twenty minutes. My sense of personal triumph lasted well into the following hour, provoking one of the secretaries into appreciative remarks about the buoyant nature of the day's correspondence. But heady moments like this were rare. More often, far more often, I was closer to tears. A man like me may be shaken to his foundations by the unwonted and unwanted business of finding himself in thrall to someone like her, someone so horribly insensitive that time and again his tears can be mistaken, falling on the very skin of her face, for mere drops of sweat. And once, when in the early morning light the cause was unmistakable, her soft, soft stroking of my back simply turned into a clumsy and indifferent patting, and she rebuked me.

'Soppy!'

I pushed the cover off, and left the bed. Thrusting my legs into my trousers, I said to her, 'I realize that, to you, an orgasm is of much the same order as a breakfast egg: it doesn't matter in the slightest who brings it to the boil. But I'm not like that!'

Snatching my shirt from the chair-back, I slammed out.

She made no effort to follow me and, after the first seething moments, I ceased to expect it. I believe I'd heard the morning news through at least twice before she ambled in, in search of the cup of tea I'd failed for once to bring to her.

'Are you all right?' she asked me, amiably enough. 'You're looking very odd.'

'I cannot pretend that our last disagreeable exchange has lifted my spirits.'

'Oh, *that*.'

Oh, *that*. How did their sensibilities become so blunted? Were we like that? Or is it too much television in early childhood? Indifferent parenting? Some as yet unsuspected side-effect of the Pill? Was she exceptional in her insensitivity? Was I too fond?

No, I was not too fond. She taught me something about love. Living with her, I learned for certain that he who loves best is best off, always. Better, I know now, to love like I did than, like her, be so well loved and yet unable to feel even a shadow of what I felt. Sometimes I pitied her, lying so contentedly beside me, physically assuaged, in every other way totally empty. At other times I felt responsible, as guilty as all those other middle-aged people in her short life who'd clearly failed her and failed her, till she could think that Passchendaele was Passiondale, and Mrs Gaskell was my cleaning lady, and love and sex were simply one and the same.

I see doubt gathering behind your eyes. You think that I malign poor little Alicia Davie. You think there must have been some feeling in the girl, she must have cared for me a little, how else could she have gone to bed time and again with such a face?

You are mistaken. But you'll make no headway into understanding unless I help you, unless I go far deeper into a side of things I now – particularly now – would rather not reflect upon; unless I'm honest with you about matters I would, had things not turned out in the way they did, have taken to the grave with me as infinitely and eternally private.

She liked my face. That was the root of it. It was macabre, and that sprang catches within her, allowing her to slip into some awful and, to me, unimaginable frame of mind in which she was at last free to feel, fully and exquisitely, sensations otherwise denied to her. Put at its bluntest, I am convinced that, till she tangled with me, Alicia Davie was little more than a sexual fake. I may, by your standards, be an inexperienced man; but I am neither ignorant nor naïve. I am aware that for many women pleasure depends upon some level of abandonment, the private creation of that harmless but enabling temporary fiction, absence of choice. I sensed early in married life the quickening excitement in Margaret when, taking weight off my own tiring body, I laid more on hers. Nor was I slow to come to recognize that forcibly stilling her body was very often the most effective way of rousing sensations within it. Lord knows what went through Margaret's mind as I made love to her. For all I know, I was transmuted into hordes of lawless teenage rapists fresh off their motorbikes, or some beefy, simple-minded cannibal with primitive notions on how to baste supper. I dread to think. But I don't have to speculate on what went through Alicia's mind, for it was written in those clear eyes she kept open all the time, stamped onto every run of her fingertips or her tongue down the grooves of my cheek and neck and shoulder, each writhing of her small body against scar tissue. No longer for Alicia the secret toils of a Frankenstein, the nightly creation within her imagination of some monster hideous enough to satisfy. She'd found a real one.

It takes some getting used to, being somebody's ghoul. It took me a while to realize that, when Alicia lit the candle on the mantelpiece, it wasn't to soften the light, or her looks, or mine; it was to carry the damn thing across and put it on the floor beside the bed on my bad side – always my bad side – so that my face, so cruelly underlit, flickered from real to surreal horror, from bogyman to vampire. 'Oh, you are *ugly*,' she'd whisper as her body twisted against the rising pressure of mine. 'You look just like a rotting corpse.'

It takes some getting used to; but I was up to it. I enjoyed it. It was a sort of game that made up for all the 'Postman's Knock' and 'Spin the Bottle' I'd missed in childhood. She'd met her match in me, as I in her. I'd push her face back hard with my spread hand, my fingers heavy on her eyelids, holding them closed. I'd puff out a cheek and squint my eyes, and twist my face into worse shapes than you can imagine. I can, of course, make faces much better than you can. I'd tell her fiercely, 'Look!' and lift my fingers from her eyelids. She'd only shudder. 'Look!' I'd say again. 'Open your eyes and look, Alicia.' And she would tremble and hesitate. Her eyelids flickered. She lacked the courage to open them. 'Come on, Alicia. Don't keep me waiting. Look!' And tears would seep between her eyelids as she opened them, and the soft tremble of her body under mine turned to a harder, more insistent, shudder, and I'd know from the very feel of her that I had given back to her the pleasure she gave me.

I never hurt her. Never once. No. Once, only once, by accident. I caught her hair under my elbow. She howled from the sudden and surprising pain. My stomach clenched into an evil knot, and then the civilized man in me was relieved beyond measure when all the excitement banked up within her dissolved into an irritable wail. 'That *hurt*. Be *careful*!' I am a moral man, and just as I cannot approve the doling out of physical pain, I cannot watch with equanimity its compliant reception. Ours was sham violence, counterfeit force. If I pulled my leather belt across the flat of her stomach, it would be fast enough to warm her skin, but not burn it. My hand lay heavy enough to whiten her skin, but not bruise. When I looped the cord of my dressing-gown around her wrists, pulled them together and up, up against the bedhead, I took care not to knot too tightly. And when, spread-eagled, she gasped, 'What if you had a heart attack?' and I whispered into the curves of her skin, 'You'd be in big trouble,' I didn't need to look up and check that she wouldn't. I am by nature a most careful man, a great believer in always leaving a little slack.

'What if you did, though? You're old, after all.'

A tightening, an increase of the pressure. 'Old, Alicia?'

'I call it old.'

'By and large, it's referred to as middle age.'

'Only by people as old, or older.' A yelp. 'No! Stop it. Stop it!'

'Hurting, my sweet?'

'No. Worried about your tiring yourself . . .'

'Are you determined to provoke me?'

'I just— No. No! Stop it now. Stop!'

'Please?'

'You've no right to—'

'You've read my books. You know that I don't hold with Rights.'

A gasp. And another. 'Oh, let me go!'

'Please?'

I gripped her to me, and forced it out of her, that wail of pleasure and surrender. 'Please, please, please, *please*.'

And I let her go. Slipped the knots from her wrists and slid her down beside me on the pillows. I ran my thumb over her damp forehead, her eyelids, the peaceful face, the smile she gave me. Brightmony crept back from temporary banishment, resettling in a coma-ridden lump against my belly, and rain beat once more against the window-panes, an old, old record, turned again.

One night, the last night of the term, she told me what I'd been expecting to hear.

'I ought to leave tomorrow. They'll be waiting for me at home.'

I pushed Brightmony farther down the bed.

'I sincerely hope that you're planning to take your cat with you.'

'Is that really all you have to say?'

'I'm afraid so.' I lay and listened to her body's murmurings, my heart still aching, the sheets of colour she'd raised in me moments before still ebbing.

'Maybe I won't bother to come back, then.'

And if you didn't, I thought, would that be so bad? I'd get along very well without you. Get straight again, have a bit of a clean-up around the flat, shift all those piles of paper banking up on my desk, and then go back to my old life. It would be a relief, of sorts, to pick up my sorely neglected research work, enjoy the odd quiet evening in front of the television, get enough sleep. Go back, in short, to reading the newspaper at leisure and growing old in peace.

'Oh, you'll be back.'

'You sound very sure.'

I rolled her over, rubbed her thin shoulders, her spine, her bottom, the little hollows at the backs of her knees.

'I am sure.'

She twisted her body round, and glared at me, feeling her dignity for the first time assailed.

'You think I couldn't leave?'

'I *know* you couldn't.'

I took her fingers in my own, and kissed them.

'How could you? You're like me, Alicia. You're not a prisoner, so you can't escape.'

Chapter 5

I felt her missing from the moment she left. As gentle and unflagging as water on pebbles, a continual purl of longing ran through me. Still on my skin like a soft touch, and in my head like a soft sound, she bruised me inside and out with her absence. You can't take a break from wanting like that.

I tried, though, believe me. Did what I could to be sensible with all the skills I have. I'd pull a chair up to my desk, draw a blank sheet of paper towards me, and, staring at it for focus of concentration, I'd try to split the debilitating stream of missing her into distinct and separate thoughts, thinking to think each one through once and only once, and have it done with. Ridiculous. And not just a simple waste of my time. These efforts I made not only lamentably failed, they also wore me out in the process. I'd perhaps manage to struggle a way through two or three semi-coherent thoughts – generally uncomplimentary to Alicia, I must say – and then the sheer sense of her would sweep over me with all the force of water undammed, and I'd be flooded with the anguish of wanting, and her not with me.

And where the hell was Brightmony, exactly? One night I searched it out on one of my old walking-maps, and, somewhat to my surprise, found the tiny, dark, irregular patches of it a few miles west of the small railway station she'd mentioned while she was cadging the train fare. I felt a little put out, seeing it there. I had, I think, not really thought in terms of Brightmony actually existing, in the same way Fort William and Glen Garry exist. Until that moment, Brightmony had meant to me little more than 'long absence'. There it was, though: faded but indisputable. I touched it with my fingertips, and the marks around it, the sheep-washes and quarries, tile-works (disused) and wells and cart tracks. I traced the edges of woods by Crook o' Burgie, admired the fine fretwork of Drummournie Lodge's glass-houses, the delicate marsh signs, the pretty meandering blue of Goat Burn. As I stood shaving next morning, missing her quiet sloshing in the bathtub beside me, names of the places around where she was rang in my ears with a tiled-bathroom echo as if I'd spoken them aloud – Bellstane and Easter Blackwood, Cotty Hole, Spindlemuir – jumbling themselves into a pottage along with Muir of this and Crofts of that, Mains of the other, Moss of something else, till I was driven back time and again to the pale, squared, canvas-backed sheet, worn thin and smooth with other handlings.

Brightmony. The thought of it grew in me like a cancer. I'd sleep with it, and wake to find it stronger than before. Brightmony. I'd take the map, fold it and prop it up against the bread tin, and stare at Brightmony on it while the toast burned. I tucked it inside the flap of my brief-case when I gathered my papers together for the day's work. I'd walk down the streets, through the cold washing rain, and feel it there, a stained and faded secret comfort. Brightmony. The secretaries looked at me strangely, and made a point of reminding me, not once, but several times, of each appointment and responsibility. They spoke up frequently, those last few working days, about their seasonal plans, looking expectantly at me as they did so, as though seeking reassurance that I, too, had people to be with and places to go over this cold, dark holiday. But I had almost lost touch with my own daily life, imagining hers. Brightmony. Brightmony. And so oblivious had I become to the general marching of days that, despite the office starling chatter of warning, I was brought up sharp one morning to find, on the far side of a strangely quiescent park, a locked door. And to my rescue came, not one of the customary servitors, but the nightwatchman, looking most out of place in broad day-light.

'Och, Professor Laidlaw, have ye nae had enough? Ye maun be unco' ta'en up wi' something to ha'e come here today!'

Uncommonly taken up, indeed. Brightmony. Bright-mony. Running the thin litany of her remarks about her home through my mind, over and over, wishing first what I knew of it less sparse, then more sparse; wishing I'd asked her more, then wishing I'd thought to clamp my hand down over her sweet mouth whenever she began to speak of it. What was it like up there in Brightmony? How did her days go? What did her father look like? What sort of woman was her mother? Were there more cats, more sisters than the one I'd heard about, any lovers? Lovers! Dear God, lovers. Imagine the myriad ways I now found to pass the time those empty festive days and nights, tormenting myself in games with no frontiers but those of the steadily warping imagination. On Christmas Day the walls and ceilings of my rooms were decorated with nothing but the twisted tinsel fancies of a man denied sleep. And so suspicion inexorably crept in the wake of fatigue. I slid from 'unco' ta'en up' to uncommonly taken down again, and farther. The man who'd planned for her absence a quiet renewal of sense and purpose, a soothing early night or two, a clear-up, went missing, and in his place there prowled around my flat a grim, unshaven and insomniac stranger whose moods swept back and forth in fierce swathes from physical longing to the most crippling attacks of self-disgust.

You see, I didn't trust her. I couldn't. It filled me with shame, but I couldn't trust her. What did I know of her? She'd lain in my bed, in my arms, as close as one can be to another, and said, 'They'll be waiting for me at home,' and I knew nothing whatever of 'home' or 'them'. I hadn't asked her. I'd taken so little interest in the rest of her life that now she was out of my flat, out of my sight, I had no way of even beginning to picture her, except in the arms of lewd country boyfriends, rustic rapist lovers.

I didn't trust her because I knew nothing about her. Could two be farther apart? She'd brought out such a fullness in me, such a rich, all-encompassing sense of being, for the first time in my life, entirely alive. She'd made my blood run and my heart beat. But I couldn't trust her, and now, with her gone, this small indifferent fact took on new life, burgeoned and grew malformed, and suddenly appeared to me proof of the vacuity of everything between us.

I had no experience in these matters. I trusted Margaret. Right to the end, I never doubted my wife for a moment. I knew, the evening she first let drop she'd lunched with a rather pleasant man from the office, that that must have been their first lunch together. When, many months later, she told me she'd just gone to bed with him, I knew it was the first, if not the last, time: Margaret would never have deceived me. And so I believed my wife when she said she was unsure whether to stay with me or go with him, just as I later took her word for it when she announced that she was sure at last, and would be leaving. Margaret's integrity was total, and I prized it dearly. I had no faith whatever in Alicia.

Doubt is a creeper. Its tendrils strangle everything it touches, present and past. Wretched already, I thought back to my former life and was made doubly wretched wondering if all that time with Margaret, all those drab years when I was only partly living and felt half dead, were not at root more real, more honest, closer even. Simply to fear the possible truth of this brought me out in a sweat. You, you've seen passion and the results of passion. You've seen the thwarted lovers twisted in death, a few last drops of weedkiller leaking insistently into the sacking on the garage floor; you've seen the man refuse to drop the gun, the woman with the knife still dripping in her hand. And you've been round next door to prise the drear and blank-faced neighbours away from their television sets with your routine enquiries. You tell me which way of living and dying is real, for I don't know. But I will tell you this much: either answer is a horror. A horror.

These were my seasonal gifts to myself: misery, distrust. And all the time I was waiting, waiting, watching the silent telephone. To banish the miles between myself and Brightmony, I read the novels she'd left about the house, trash though they were. I washed a lone sock of hers by hand, and aired it tenderly. I kept one of my shirts that somehow smelled of her body under the pillow for comfort. I even squandered hours that would have been far better spent addressing my energies to my own work in looking up recondite facts for the essay Brown had rather unseasonably set her to write over the holiday period.

I saw the New Year in alone, and there was nothing mellow about my reflections, or anything laudable in my resolutions. I spent the evening in my armchair, humming the same tune softly, over and over, swaying the whisky glass to time. Reminded by absence of former presences, I watched the clock hands creep around and thought of how Margaret at this time each year would be perched on the very edge of the empty chair opposite me now, glancing continually at the clock and wondering when to make the obligatory telephone call to her mother. Each New Year's Eve the same two propositions were disinterred for another appraisal: the closer to midnight the call, the more festive; but, on the other hand, the closer to midnight, the greater the likelihood of her finding herself thwarted by busy lines south. Each year, emboldened by two small celebratory whiskies, Margaret would appeal to me for my advice. Each year I shook my head and declined to give it.

'Maybe I shouldn't wait. She might not bother to stay up. She doesn't every year. She might be halfway into bed by now. What do you think?'

I myself found the very notion of Margaret's mother preparing for bed entirely repellent. But general consideration of this scenario would keep Margaret occupied on and off until about half past ten, the time at which she always cracked and made the call. (I say always; but I've known her give in as early as nine, and once, distracted by baking for a New Year's Day charity lunch, she managed to hold out till five to eleven.) She'd slip off her chair, saying a little guiltily, 'I think I'll phone her now. I don't *think* it's too early.' And a few moments later she'd be calling over to me in cheery astonishment from where she stood beside the telephone table, 'I'm getting through! I think – yes! – it's ringing!'

Surprise, surprise. And then there was the call itself, always good for twenty minutes, or even longer. Then chewing over the cud of news from her mother. It all filled the gap nicely between half past ten and a couple of minutes before it struck midnight. I'd rise to pour a drop more whisky into her glass. ('No, Ian. No! Well, just a sip to toast. It *is* New Year!') I'd stretch my wrist, and my exposed watch-face provoked her into a traditional last-minute twitter: her wristwatch fast, perhaps; mine spot on, she expected, as usual; the clock on the mantelpiece had never been trustworthy since that shoddy overhaul at Callaghan's. And then, at last, the merciful bells outside were heard to chime, apparently taking her quite by surprise as usual. A gay, festive sip on her part, one last anaesthetizing slug on my own, and the whole grisly business was over, thank God, for yet another year. Are other marriages like this? Do other grown men and women regularly eke out such tiresome evenings, willing on clock hands, longing for bed and dark and privacy? Within two years of getting married I had invented for myself a private game, played almost till the day that Margaret left me, by which I secretly awarded myself one point each time that I successfully headed her away from one of her stock remarks, her knee-jerk responses, and, more perversely perhaps, double points for successfully steering her towards one. It wasn't a demanding pastime. Margaret's mind, trained over long years of living alone with her mother, was no rich and fertile wilderness but rather a set of drab and thinly planted flowerbeds far too well kept to permit anything more unexpected than a little restrained reseeding. If at any time between December and February I were to remark on the bitterness of the weather, she would be bound to ask, 'If Winter comes, can Spring be far behind?' If I spoke of fatigue, she'd come straight back, 'Better to wear out than rust out.' Each conversation had its official conclusion: 'Still, I mustn't say more. She's always been very nice to me.' 'It's over now and done with. No point in fretting.' 'All the same really, aren't they, people?' Saying these things made her feel more secure. She was comfortable with the familiar and trivial. If we went for a walk, I'd welcome sharp, cold air into my lungs, and stride with all the more vigour because, under great scudding clouds, the huge earth seemed to roll perceptibly. She'd scurry in my wake, distracted by all manner of pastoral minutiae. I had no time for some bud sitting on the end of a twig here, a bird squawk there, hedgehogs. It was mere naming of parts, Margaret's way of seeing the world small, protecting herself from the sheer majesty of land and sea and sky. She had no real interest in natural science. She'd hold me up for minutes on end standing and wondering about the habits of foxes. I never saw her take a book on the topic out of the local library. Margaret's knowledge of country matters comprised little more than a handful of keepsakes culled from those few Sunday walks with her father that studded an otherwise cheerless childhood.

If he'd lived longer she might have learned more, perhaps developed a deep and rewarding interest. But he was driven to his grave before poor Margaret's seventh birthday, leaving her entirely at the mercy of her mother. You'll gather I was never over-fond of Mother-in-law, a rancorous woman of complex and lasting grudges who could spy faults with her eyes closed. We got on badly from the first. I took particularly against her rather cunning stratagem for trying to disguise her ignorance – that of despising everything in the world about which she knew little or nothing – and she, acting purely out of self-interest, did her fiendish best to stop her daughter marrying me. She wanted Margaret for herself. And being both criminally manipulative and an accomplished liar, the selfish old bat managed to keep up the lonely widow theme until the very wedding day, then astonish everyone by getting remarried herself fewer than six weeks later in the same church.

Yes, we were married in church. It was a strained affair, I must admit, with two or three senile great-uncles sitting uncomfortably in the front pew hankering for lavatories, and the bride's mother visibly sulking. But Margaret insisted. She was a Roman Catholic then, though I can't recall she kept that up for any appreciable length of time after the wedding. It can't, thinking back, have been easy for Margaret. Oh, I'd gone along with her tearful request for a wedding in church, seeing it as of no more significance than any other voodoo form of union. But I had, deep down, resented very strongly the most disreputable way in which the Roman church takes advantage at a susceptible moment and makes the unbelieving partner promise in writing not to stand in the way of the indoctrination of his own offspring with the very same warped and limiting credo. For Margaret's sake, and with no intention of ever having children, I signed. But it was in the deepest spirit of indignation. And I suspect that it was partly due to this that I embarked upon a series of caustic attacks on her beliefs and practices that caused her first to attempt to argue feebly back at me, frequently weeping with frustration, then to become tense and secretive about her spiritual life, and finally to lose her faith. I wasn't proud of this, you understand. It was no triumph on my part – though, given the tenets of that faith, no loss on hers, either. Arguing is one of the more basic of my professional skills. Ask me to argue black is white and I will make a better job of it than Margaret arguing black is black. Far better. No, it can't have been easy, living with me. I find it hard to drop the abstract in favour of the comforting or personal. If I took Margaret to the cinema and she enjoyed the film, the whole remembrance of it might be ruined for her for ever by my making one or two slightly analytical observations about it on the way down the carpeted steps to the foyer, and our occasional evenings of bridge with the Browns had to be shelved after my discussion on the walk home of some of the hands played had upset Margaret once or twice rather too badly. To tell the truth, I've never really understood how other couples 'just get along'. I suspect that, for starters, the women know better than to tangle with my sort.

But I was not unkind. I did my best. I gave Margaret steady support through all the little difficulties with her health, and the vicissitudes of her job, and the fortnightly afternoon teas with her mother. This last was no small sacrifice on my part, I assure you, involving me as it did in years of social contact with her new stepfather, a man whom I disliked quite as thoroughly as everyone else including, so far as I could make out, Margaret's mother. Then, mercifully, one afternoon this repellent old man made the serious strategic error of making a pathetic little pass at my Margaret while searching for Jaffa cakes deep in the larder. There was much talk of deleterious side-effects from some drug he was taking at the time for his prostate; but I'd have none of that. It was all the excuse I needed. The break was made at my insistence.

And after a welcome period of estrangement that loosened the apron-strings once and for all, contact between the two homes was at last reduced to the occasional festive telephone call and, when the old lady's hypochondria was in its more rampant phases, the odd brief sick visit.

I don't know if Margaret missed having contact with her mother. I never thought to ask. She had her job (she was a grading officer), the house and me. It is true that shortly after this unpleasant rift she had to stop work for a month or two with some amorphous combination of symptoms, plainly of psychosomatic origin. The doctor gave her pills and she obediently swallowed them. I can't say that they served much purpose. I didn't think they would. I tend to take the view that one doctor simply makes work for another, and so was not overly surprised when after several weeks had passed she was still weepy and listless. I took over all the cleaning and shopping and cooking. I was quite pleased to have the opportunity. One can reflect whilst one vacuums and polishes. He who shops gets to exercise his preferences and, as for the cooking, it was a great relief to me to be allowed, under the guise of an invalid menu, to introduce steaming and poaching into a kitchen routine largely based on her mother's, where stewing and frying had been for far too long the rather indigestible mainstays.

Margaret got better gradually; but still I managed to hang on to all my new duties. I was reluctant to relinquish them. The flat was better kept, our diet more varied, and my stomach and bowels less frequently placed under strain than before. Margaret may well have felt herself a little displaced. In the last couple of weeks before she took up work again she did go round the flat attempting to reassure herself that she was no longer a domestic passenger. She moved the lighter items of furniture around. She rearranged linen in the airing cupboard. She put the spices into alphabetical order. I tried to be supportive. But it is trying to trip over stools set down in unaccustomed places, to have to root for a clean handkerchief, to reach out for dried thyme and lay one's hand on rennet tablets. I think Margaret noticed my irritation. I think it upset her. Certainly it was about this time she started doing some very strange things. One day, without a word's warning, she came home with her hair so coarsely and unattractively cropped that it was weeks before she looked herself again. Another time she flew at me in the street, enraged about the speed at which I was walking. And one night she doused herself in perfume and sat in bed wearing a glossy nightdress I'd not seen before – not at all her style, and hardly the thing for our inclement winters. I didn't say a thing, but when I went in turn to the bathroom it was, I think, no accident that I noticed the absence of those faint, tell-tale smears on the cabinet mirror, those little cream-smudged finger-prints that I had always tended to associate with Margaret's demonstrations of sexual affection.

I coughed to disguise in so far as I could the tiny click of the ball-bearing catch as I pulled the medicine cabinet open. On the top shelf I found the pale blue plastic shell that housed her contraceptive diaphragm. It was still there, still sleeping inside, dusted over with talcum powder and clearly unwanted on this particular evening.

But I was wanted, that was also clear. Margaret's arms reached out without delay or hesitation. The glossy new nightdress rucked up against my belly, feeling strange, and she offered her mouth far more willingly than usual.

I kissed her. Of course I kissed her. I was as tender as I could be. I held her close and rocked her in her need, and even went some way towards offering her what physical satisfaction I could. I did my best for her, but I would not make love that night. In my mind's eye that small, complacent, dusty diaphragm sat in its plastic box and mocked me, conspiring with Margaret's deep need, and the dishonourable contract I so regretted having signed for our wedding, and the two parish priests I ordered from the house after some gross impertinence about our lack of marital fecundity. I was tender, yes, but could not give her what I knew she wanted. She cried. Of course she cried. Women will always weep about these things. I left the room, but still I heard her crying through the wall, or thought I did, right through a sleepless night till morning. At breakfast she sat without appetite, her eyes red-rimmed, her skin blotched and bloated. I half expected her to stay at home that day; but no, at fifteen minutes past eight she set off for her work as usual. When I returned from the university that evening, her eyes were no longer swollen, her skin had lost that puffy look, and nothing more was said on the matter. She was reserved in bed for quite a while. The little diaphragm stayed in its box. But then one night, brushing my teeth, I noticed two smeared fingerprints on the bright mirror. I took the trouble to shave. I brushed my hair. And when I joined

96

her in the bed and reached out for her with the greatest relief, she stroked my good cheek and came to me without reluctance. Once again, we were man and wife.

But I think it was no more than a few weeks after this that Margaret conceived the notion of getting a dog. She started off by talking about how other people she knew kept little dogs in flats like ours. She noticed favoured breeds in the street. She read out snippets from the pet columns in the local paper. Once she even mentioned the possibility of our moving to a ground-floor flat with garden access. I can't say I was keen. Nor that I felt the slightest pang of regret when the idea finally shrivelled and died for want of my encouragement. But one day I returned from work to find a startling addition to the furnishings: a large glass tank sitting on top of the refrigerator, and in it, endlessly swimming round and round, two identical goldfish.

I cannot easily explain quite why those two goldfish so disturbed me. They came in January when the winter light can pierce the kitchen. I'd raise my eyes from morning toast to catch a fierce glint of orange as one or other of them rounded the little copse of greenery with which my Margaret had thoughtfully furnished them. I'd watch their ceaseless, shimmering circling, their sinuous twists and turns, their soft, gleaming-bellied forays to the surface, their silent probings of the four sides of hard glass that were to keep the two of them hemmed in till death, and I'd regard my wife with real disquiet. Was this how Margaret felt? Were they suffering? Was she? There was some element of fellow-feeling, certainly. How else could she have learned to tell the two of them apart? Why had she brought these glimmering interlopers into our kitchen, except as a rebuke to me that all the motions of her own life had come to her to seem as pointless, her experiences as thin, her future as bleak?

From the day she imported those fish, I tried harder. Though it made quite a dent in my schedule, I accompanied her every now and again to lunch at the staff club. I took more of an interest in her work. I bought her flowers regularly. But I can't say I was surprised to lose her to another man. It seems to me our marriage was a mistake from the start. I had not chosen right and neither had she. Coming from the unfortunate home she had, she could forgive herself for any such miscalculation. It's not so easy to exonerate myself. When you've a face like mine it should be obvious, even in periods of intense desire and loneliness, that absence of real choice is more than likely to result in gross and desperate error. I should have taken more care. I blame myself. But people marry wrongly all the time. The sin lies not in that but in compounding all the foolishness by failing to show sufficient moral strength afterwards to lay aside all the temptations of distraction and excuses and set about that gruelling lifetime enterprise of joint reconstruction that makes an ill-matched couple shake down into a Darby and Joan. Here again I must hold Margaret quite blameless. She was too weak and limited in vision, and far, far too intimidated by me, to embark without direction and encouragement on such a long haul. If we made nothing of our union the fault was mine entirely. I was too busy.

She was quite right to cut out in the end. I bear no grudge – indeed, wish for her sake she'd done it sooner. I have to say that when she left, taking the goldfish with her, I felt little more than relief that guilt at all my marital shortcomings would be no longer an intrinsic part of meals eaten at my own kitchen table. And when she telephoned on some slight pretext, as she so kindly did several times in those first few days of our separation, I'd have to watch my tone of voice, take care I did not hurt her feelings by allowing myself to sound as sanguine as I felt about my sudden change of circumstances. One morning, a few weeks after our parting, she called me at the university, taking me somewhat by surprise. Margaret? The line was fuzzy and my mind went blank. 'Margaret!' My very cordiality gave me away. And though the phone call was entirely civil, she certainly excused herself a good deal more promptly than usual and didn't ring for several weeks. As soon as I realized I called her, a little concerned, at the number she now shared with my successor. She came to the telephone readily enough when informed who it was at the end of the line, and she sounded pleasant enough. Still, I detected some new element of reserve in her tone, and found it a little irritating that she seemed unable for the length of our conversation to shed the notion that I must have had some specific reason for getting in touch. This hurt my feelings and I did not phone again, though I was tempted once or twice. There was no contact between us at all until the following New Year's Eve, when she rang me. And as I heard her voice wishing me seasonal greetings, and quite inadvertently glanced at my watch-face to see that it was only five past ten, I realized with a bit of a pang that more strings had untied for Margaret, and I'd been relegated to a position in her life of slightly less importance than that of her mother.

Water runs under bridges. That's what New Year is for, isn't it, to sit alone with the whisky watching a phone that doesn't ring, and thinking about what's gone for good, and what's come along to fill the raw places. At five to ten I lifted the telephone receiver from its cradle and laid it gently on the table top, replacing it only at eleven fifteen when I was quite sure I'd be safe from Margaret. The last hour passed. Alicia didn't ring. From time to time the obstinate little tune in my head broke through the scum of love's green sickness into a patch of audibility, and it was at one of these moments I realized it was a tune of no small significance I was humming, belonging as it did to a song called 'Suspicion'. Do you recall it? 'Suspicion, suspicion, it's got its hold on me'? One heard it often enough on the wireless during the fifties. Though I'm still familiar with the melody, I can't remember much more than those few words, and that the young lady in question walks from the dance floor with a ladder running right down the back of one of her stockings, only to reappear some time later with the very same ladder still plainly visible, but this time running down the other leg. 'Suspicion, suspicion,' her lover sings, 'it's got its hold on me.' And dead right, too. I wasn't humming it again after a break of thirty years for nothing. What was she doing that she couldn't take a moment to ring me? I thought about it for a little while longer, and suddenly it came to me that, just like everyone else in the city that night, Professor Ian Laidlaw had somewhere to go.

*　　*　　*

100

It was a vile night. Rain pitched down from dark layers of sky. Cars, police vans, and even the occasional late bus hurled wide sheets of gutter water up from their wheels as they passed. Before I'd gone the length of the street, my trouser legs were drenched and clinging. On the corner a man stood in the shelter of a doorway playing the pipes, a sound acceptable enough with swaying kilts and a strong purpose, dismal in wet and cold and dark. Passing firstfooters called their greeting out to him. I strode by in silence.

I took the route across the park, glad of the darkness, grateful both for the stretching of my legs and spine, and for the taste of cold, wet air after the evening's stuffy, soft imprisonment. My eyes played tricks on me. I stepped in dog dirt and scraped my ankle against a fallen lump of bark. As I drew near the park's black, sodden centre the sense swept over me of having left behind, not just the city lights, but city time and city order. Twice I stopped, listening to the roar of wind and rain, and once I saw a dog cross from one shadowy place to another, its long, slim muzzle and mask caught in what little light there was. It glided over the path in front of me and disappeared in a streak. I looked around but could see no-one with it. It might have been a wolf at liberty, going its own way in the city at night. And though over the years of passing dogs like him in streets and parks I've come to terms with that sleek shape, those black and knowing eyes, that padding danger, still the hair on the undamaged side of the nape of my neck rose as he passed by, and I could feel again the cold, gritty damp of the wall I was leaning my chin on the moment the chain snapped and that crazed, snarling creature leaped up and over to wreathe my still grinning face in sickening breath, stifle my screams and rip me down.

The park may have been empty except for the visitation of ancient phantoms, but the city centre seemed lively enough when I finally reached it. I strode along, past brightly lit shops stuffed with seasonal goodies. Another mile, and these gave way to dark lines of terraced houses with the occasional tinsel Christmas tree standing forlorn in the window, twinkles all switched off in the miserable half-light. Rain stippled puddles and gutters. Drunks seemed thicker on the ground and more insistent in their geniality the closer I came to my destination. One backed from a narrow alley ineptly fumbling at his trouser buttons and reeled straight into me. I seized him by the elbows and pushed him back. Mistaking the strength of my grip on him for seasonal cordiality, he wished me well and would have lunged towards me once again for a fraternal hug had not the headlamps from a passing car suddenly lit up my face. A pair we must have looked there, he and I: a stupid, lurching bundle staring in sobering shock at a livid horror. As I pushed by, he shook his head and whispered 'Nae sae guid, nae sae guid' at me, and stared, frankly appalled, as I passed him.

I'm not the man to put the damper on anyone's Hogmanay. After this incident, I took to crossing streets whenever anyone appeared in front of me, and I continued across the city in this zig-zag fashion until I finally found myself under the very same street lamp where only weeks ago I had resolved with such determination never again to walk down Ardmory Road.

I slowed my pace in walking past the house. It was quite dark. Not so much as a crack of light showed through the windows, front or sides. I walked on as far as the shop on the corner, then turned, retracing my steps, but this time as I reached the house I sidestepped smartly in through the broken gateway, then fairly crept along the narrow path until I was standing beside her window.

I don't for the life of me know what I thought I would find. I pushed my face up hard against the glass, and peered inside. I stared and stared, and with the help of what I remembered from my first visit, gradually the large black shadows took shape – that was the bed and that the chair; desk and shelves over against that wall there; a mirror. And then, as my eyes became more and more accustomed to the absence of light, I could see everything clearly, as she had left it when she last strolled out through the door. What was I looking for, for God's sake? Did I expect to see two mugs still steaming on the table? Cinema ticket stubs from that afternoon's show? An unused rail ticket to Brightmony? What did I want? I didn't know, but one thing was certain. She wasn't in there, disporting herself in the bed with another. And whatever it was I wanted, I wasn't going to find it standing outside.

And if there were a turning-point, then this was it. I'm not a fool. I know as well as you there's all the difference in the world between feeling one might be justifiably aggrieved, and feeling one might be justified in committing a grievance. It's neither a fine distinction nor awkward to grasp. Granted my faculties were dulled by distress and lack of sleep, but one would have to be a

103

congenital idiot not to take the distinction on board. Even Scott-Watson would have handled it without any trouble, and I can't see it holding up Alasdair Mackie for more than a couple of moments. But I, I ran aground on it. I scuttled my integrity on its shallow reef – no mean feat, I assure you, professionally speaking. Clear thinking is, after all, fundamental to my profession. To you in yours, the end result – my forcing of Alicia's door – may sound a trivial enough matter. For me, it was an act of personal shipwreck. For when I say it was the turning-point I mean that, had you at any time in my life before that moment asked, 'Ian Laidlaw, are you an honourable man?' I would have answered you, 'I am'. Now, if you were, unkindly, to ask the same question, I'd stir uneasily and find it very hard to reply. And that has made all the difference.

It wasn't a difficult house to break into. Or maybe I've just seen enough of your public-service announcements warning against housebreakers to know how it's done. I snapped the lock, but since it was clearly irresponsibly in-effective I wasn't going to start feeling sorry about that. I closed the door behind me, pulled down the blind, switched on the light, and stood in the middle of her squalid little room, wondering where on earth to begin.

It took well over an hour to go through her things – all her things. I missed out nothing, I assure you. Went through her cupboards, shelves and boxes. Tangled my fingers in the elastic of her underwear searching the backs of her drawers; rubbed the ends of my fingers raw flip-ping through pages of her books, looking for tell-tale slips of paper; filthied my trousers with dust and fluff picked up rooting beneath her bed. I prised the tops off tins stacked behind her tiny electric oven, checked through the food packets and under the cutlery tray, looked in the teapot. I lifted her bedside lamp, and even pulled drawing-pins from the corners of all her posters to see if she'd tucked anything away behind them. I rolled back loose flaps of carpet, examined the lamp-shade, heaved up the mattress to peer beneath it and even rolled the window-blind down farther, to the very end, to see if anything fell out.

Nothing. Nowhere. Drew, as your transatlantic counterparts are reputed to say, a complete blank. Time to go home, lighter in spirits, wouldn't you think? Failure to find something you dread to find should surely be viewed as a kind of success.

But not by me. Oh, no. I just felt cheated. Standing there in the detritus of her daily life, her revolting habits, I suddenly realized that I was no longer after relief from mistrust. I was not in the running for reassurance. Quite the reverse. I was disappointed. Thwarted, even. I'd wanted to find something – anything – any thin cobweb strand of evidence to justify continuing suspicion. That's what I'd left my warm fireside and crossed the city in the filthy wet and broken into her room to find. Nothing less. Not only that, but it was clear from my disgruntlement that in not finding it a chance to feel something far more important to me than simple relief or reassurance had somehow slipped away between my fingers.

What, though? The urge to bash her? The inclination to punch her lights out for dishonesty? Dear God, no! Please, not that! But it was something vile, that much I knew. I had no doubt. I felt it inside me. I even saw it. When I looked up into her mirror, I saw reflected a new betrayal. Where, before, Ugliness – a spectre with whom I'm perfectly familiar – used to stand alone, now Ignominy stood at his side, and both stared insolently back, as though they dared me to do something, anything at all, to satisfy the adder inside me that Alicia's absence had woken from a lifetime of sleep.

I turned to go. As quickly as I could, I made for the door, and in so doing found what I'd spent an hour both looking for and overlooking. The handle I turned was on the wrong door. This was a cupboard, and since its door mirrored exactly the one through which I'd entered her room, in my frantic searching I'd not noticed its existence. Until I pulled it open, purely by accident, I'd no idea that it was there. But so it was, and piled so high with stuff I had to put a hand out to stop some of the more unsteady articles falling out on top of me. Everything was stacked in the untidiest of heaps. Even large boxes, which could have been neatly placed one on top of the other, had just been shoved in any old way. I thought it typical of Alicia's slovenliness, until I realized that none of it was hers. It was all climbing gear. There it lay, piled all haphazard – ropes, chains, pitons and crampons, snap-links and harnesses, water-bottles, boxes of dehydrated foodstuffs, bundles of flares, a moth-eaten balaclava, piles of maps, climbing boots, helmets. And every carton had on its side, stencilled in large red letters, the name ALLAN WARNER.

You want to know exactly what I took, don't you? You want a precise inventory. Very well. A bit of rope, quite

106

frayed in places; some lengths of slim steel chain and a dozen or so of those karabiners – I think that's what they're called – the small steel things that look like little figures-of-eight. Some had snap-locks and some spring-loaded gates. Nothing else. I'd be astonished if Warner even noticed anything had gone. The cupboard was a mess. I left it almost as full as I found it, and that was pretty full, I assure you. I don't know why anyone would want to climb up a mountain carrying all that stuff. No, I'm not interested in mountain- or rock-climbing, and never have been. No, I had no intention whatsoever of taking either up as a hobby. Yes, yes, I do admit I had a very clear idea indeed of how I planned to use what I'd taken. Yes, yes, I did. I do admit it.

She came back seven nights later. Stood in the half-dark of the stairwell, her stuffed-to-bursting overnight bag slung over her shoulder, her cat in a cardboard box at her feet. Cross-patch with tiredness, unsure of her reception, she was, she said stiffly, perfectly happy to go on down to Ardmory Road, if that was more 'convenient'.

'Come in,' I told her. 'Come in, Alicia.'

My time of waiting was over.

Chapter 6

So term began, like any other. Within the offices and corridors, the students expressed their customary dissatisfaction with a restored and genial rudeness in place of that rather dispiriting whining that tends to prevail towards the end of a term. My colleagues reappeared wearing new ties which the secretaries took time off to admire. In return, my colleagues exclaimed over the hydrangea's holiday growth-spurt. Everyone, including me, had nothing but praise for the freshly painted woodwork. Of course there were dampers. Brown took a bit of consoling after the sudden cancellation of his course Differentiated Fiscal Statuses for Peripheral Regions because of an enrolment figure of one; and there was a tone of unprecedented menace in the Dean's memorandum on the paucity of volunteers for Extra-Mural Studies. But, these things apart, all was sweetness and light. I sat at my desk in the bright winter sunlight and worked with ease and dispatch, pleasure even, deciding, organizing, delegating duties, arranging the departmental meetings. The secretaries moved busily and contentedly between the two offices, relieved to find me my old self again, and satisfied with my renewed efficiency as I worked steadily through each day, dictating and signing the letters, initialling the constant stream of memoranda, and soothing the ruffled feathers of colleagues fussed by one or another of the petty personal antagonisms common to any university faculty. I was the perfect head of department, reeling off references, making distant lunch-dates with the neglected, taking a mental note of the names sent along from the Student Health Centre on little white slips—

Well, look at that. A little white slip – *the* little white slip. I take my hat off to you, truly I do. You're quicker, in every sense, than I gave you credit for, and be assured I took you from the start for no man's fool. I do no more than mention little white slips in passing, and there you go rooting in your briefcase, and out one comes. You lay it on the table between us like a receipt for a thunderbolt. Exhibit B. Tell me, do all such objects come to look so very inoffensive directly after the offence? Should we digress for a moment here to talk man to man, philosophically, about the banality of evil? No, perhaps not. Time's getting on, and we should too. But I admit you've shaken me for the moment. I think I'll ask my secretary to fetch some coffee, perhaps a sandwich or two. I do think sending out for a snack would prove far simpler than your escorting me to the staff club cafeteria. Though

I don't know. You're clearly a resourceful fellow. What else have you got tucked away in that briefcase? Enough Exhibit A snap-locks and lengths of chain to take me along with you, should you prefer to lunch out?

I'm sorry. That was quite uncalled for. I do apologize. Give me a small moment, would you? Perhaps you'd take the opportunity to mention that coffee to whichever of the secretaries is still tapping away out there . . . Thank you . . . Thank you . . .

Right, then. The little white slip. Now let me see. It must have surfaced no more than two or three weeks into the term. It's dated the twenty-seventh of January, and I've no reason to suppose it took more than a couple of days to get to us from the Student Health Centre. It was a Thursday, that I do recall, because on Thursdays I take the Comparative Government seminar. You can pin down the date quite easily, since it was one of those Thursdays on which Scott-Watson was present – a bit of a rarity, as I think I've had occasion to mention. Certainly I took the opportunity of handing back to him a couple of his shoddy pieces of work, and attributing their poor quality, at least in part, to his somewhat fitful attendance.

'Mine?' he said. '*Mine?*' He gazed round at the others, trawling for moral support in his outrage. 'I don't know why you're getting at me. I've come as often as the next man.'

I gently indicated the seating arrangements.

'I am the next man,' I pointed out. 'And you have come nowhere near as often as I have.'

Alicia spurted with mirth. Warner chuckled.

MacFaddyen looked anxious, as though she feared Scott-Watson and I might fall to open quarrelling. McKinley continued to stare vacantly out of the window. I doubt if he even heard the exchange.

Scott-Watson huffed and humped about in his chair, muttering in a most sullen fashion, taking his time to settle into the topic in hand. Outside, snow fell for the first time that winter – there, there's another clue to the date, should you have contacts within the Meteorological Office – and it distracted them horribly. They're children still, really. The first snowfall, thunder bangs, lightning, very heavy rain – all these things cause them to become physically restless, impossible to teach. I pressed on, though. It is my job. I was attempting to din into their misted minds the notion of a wide discrepancy between the principles enshrined in written consti-tutions, and actual governmental practices. Over the years I've found it's less any vague, ideological leanings they may be trammelled with that impede their ability to grasp this really rather simple idea, more their utter lack of cognizance that out there is a real world, real people doing real jobs, bureaucracies functioning in their own small ways, day after day, with little more than the oc-casional nod and a wink towards the theories that supposedly inform their routine. This innocence of theirs appals me. It makes me shudder for their eventual employers. I'm actually astonished there hasn't been more of a backlash over the years, unless you interpret the new technological revolution as an attempt to rid some industries of the need to employ quite so many of them. Warner picked at his nails. Alicia daydreamed and, kindly, I left her to it since she was as short on sleep as I was. Scott-Watson continued to sulk, MacFaddyen to worry. When, trying to stir up the bones in this graveyard of intellectual endeavour, I mentioned a recent and particularly murderous outrage by the Soviet Government that served, I thought, rather neatly to illustrate the point I was making, MacFaddyen only looped the chain of her crucifix more tightly around the peace badge pinned upside down on her woolly, and said to me very anxiously indeed, 'I'm sure the Russians didn't really mean it.'

Now few of MacFaddyen's seminar contributions are drawn from the cutting-edge of radical thought; but none the less, at times like this the suspicion that I am gravely underpaid does tend to flit across the mind, causing a momentary distraction.

It was, unusually, Alicia who broke the silence.

'It makes no difference if they're thugs or fools,' she scolded MacFaddyen. 'It's still terrifying.' She turned to me for my approval. 'Isn't that right?'

Discomfited by her sheer intimacy of tone, I rose and moved across to the window.

'Certainly,' I said, pretending to look out at falling snow. 'Either circumstance would give justifiable rise to some apprehension.'

I turned back to catch, unmistakably, a smile passing between Alicia and Warner. They smoothed out their expressions to innocence fast, but not quite fast enough. I'd seen them.

To disguise my vexation, I reached for Dolgorov and Volstein, on the top shelf. Scott-Watson took the opportunity of my back being turned to lean across and snarl under his breath at Alicia, 'You weren't talking that way this morning, were you? I reckon you have as many political opinions at one time as you have—'

The adder stirred. Whether it was the look on my face as I swung round, or whether it was some last vestige of discretion within his disagreeable nature that stopped him short there, I shall never know. But, very wisely, he fell silent.

MacFaddyen squirmed. She hates unpleasantness and felt, quite rightly, that she was in some way to blame.

'The Russians aren't the only ones,' she said, coming to what she may, in the heat of the moment, have mistaken for rescue. 'There's—'

She paused, plumbing the depths of her ill-informed mind for some matching outrage, some twin in all but ideological shading. It is an awesome tribute to her ignorance that she failed to find one. More out of pity than interest, Warner supplied her with some example culled from Latin America, but this proved to be a serious error of judgement on his part, for McKinley promptly woke up. McKinley fancied himself an authority on all right-wing governments in that hemisphere ever since his elder brother came back from the Falklands alive and crowing. He and Scott-Watson fell at once to bickering. The names of countries not noted for their libertarian tendencies began to fly about the room, familiar tennis-balls worn thin in the jejune game of political recrimination. Alicia and Warner eyed one another, and, more covertly, me, with increasing unease as the seminar degenerated around us; but I, I turned my back on all of them, and, resting my burning cheek on the cold, soothing window glass, stared out for comfort.

Snow was still falling. Outside, the familiar view of tower blocks and trees and squares and pathways was silently slipping away into a pure and whitened world, the winter gift, the poignant perennial reminder of an un-sullied earth. For the first time in very many years, I thought of my childhood. A memory suddenly came back to me of pressing my face hard up against just such a chilly windowpane to watch the snow fall and blanket my domain, of seeing the strange, white stilling of dull bushes into alarming shapes, the magical vanishing of over-familiar trees into such glistening filigree play-grounds as I would have sold my soul to be permitted to climb in the cold, blue dusk-light. And I recalled leaning back on the narrow window-ledge to ease the sharpening pins and needles, and seeing quite plainly in dark, reflecting glass, my own face. Not this one. Not this mess. The other. The long-forgotten, unremarkable face that only came to light again in photographs found hidden in a drawer after my mother's funeral. My first face. The face I had before – as I with sudden fierce clarity remembered thinking it – before my mother told the people in the hospital to take me away and make me a monster.

Voices behind me, lifting in anger, fetched me back over more than forty years. McKinley and Scott-Watson, it seemed, had worked their way no farther down the Shibboleth Fixture List than Chile v. Afghanistan. Pulling the wrangle that had developed back into some profitable form of discussion was out of the question. I'd lost the concentration and lost the will. To cut things short, I lifted a pile of reading-lists down from the shelf and

115

handed them round, to the customary accompaniment of resentful squawking.

'Not now,' I told them. 'I don't want to hear it. Hush up, the lot of you. Go home.'

Obediently, they gathered up their things, stuffing their dog-eared notepads away, picking their grubby scarves off the floor. Alicia moved slowly, slower than the others. Clearly she planned to stay behind and make a speech in her defence against Scott-Watson's potentially scabrous allegation. It was the last thing in the world I wanted to hear. Without a word, I slipped directly through the connecting door into the secretaries' office, and locked it behind me.

The room was empty. It was well after five. I sat in the swivel chair in front of the shrouded typewriter and waited while the last grumbles faded in the corridor. I waited till Alicia's verminous little scrabblings on the door had ceased, and her footfalls, too, had died away. Only when it was perfectly safe, and perfectly quiet, did I allow myself to hear again, run with the accuracy of a tape-recording, 'I reckon you have as many political opinions at one time as you have—'

What? Bras? Pretty knickers? Library books? Or lovers? Warner, of course. Live in a cramped little rathole like 18A Ardmory Road, and you don't continue to lend out an entire storage cupboard simply for old times' sake. Was it possible, though? Was that really what she'd been up to all those times she'd ambled back into the flat so much later than expected, and in such a gentle, quiet mood that I'd suspected her of dabbling with drugs? Was it Warner's sexual prowess I had to thank for all those

116

restful evenings and peaceful suppers, and, now I came to reflect on it, those nights of early and unbroken sleep?

The mere thought was sufficient to sicken me. And, make no mistake, this was no longer simple jealousy. Come, I'd developed some resistance to that. I had, after all, caught that one – the most common of the adult diseases – conveniently over the break, and I remembered only too well what that one felt like. No, this was some new virus, and one against which my body had clearly built up far fewer defences. This was humiliation. Now I'm not saying she'd humiliated me. That isn't what I mean at all. What did it matter if, from time to time, Alicia still slept with Warner? She never said she loved me. I didn't own her. In any event, swapping close friends about is right and fitting behaviour in the young, and if along with this come inconvenient periods of overlapping sexual entanglement, then so be it. The worst of the traditional disasters no longer attend such mores, and I'm not a man to preach a set of ethics I regard with misgiving simply because it would salve my false pride. So I won't claim that she'd humiliated me. How could the self-esteem of someone of my age depend on the sexual constancy of someone of hers? But she had been the cause of my humiliation. Oh, yes, she had. Try to imagine what it means to a man like me to feel his mind go numb and his innards churn because, midway through a seminar of mind-cracking tedium, some blurted half-of-an-insult has suddenly brought home to him in force that he's in thrall to someone like her, someone so negligent, so easy come – 'With me?' – so easy go – 'I'm perfectly happy to go on down to Ardmory Road, if that's more convenient'

– that he can hold himself no more than one in a bunch of the most careless personal relationships. Indifference is the worst of provocations, and I'm not used to it. No-one has ever treated me like that. No-one. I told you, people are different to me. In my sheer hideousness resides my distinction. People defer to it. They treat my scarring with respect. I'm not just one more fellow in a line. I am special.

But not to her. Not to Alicia. She was set fair to sail, in her insensitive and thoughtless way, through the last barrier. How had the line of lovers gone before I happened along? Just running through the possibilities furnished by one small seminar group made the mind boggle. Warner, for sure. How about McKinley? Yes, what was McKinley thinking about as he stared so morosely out of the window? And, God forbid, Scott-Watson. Alicia's sex-life could hardly be a matter of indifference to him, to judge from the pique behind his attack. Had he, perhaps, resented having to make way for Allan Warner, who, in his turn, lost out a little to Ian Laidlaw – oh, just another lover, suiting her in some ways: his flat was warm, his food was good, he gave her a bit of help with her studies; but no doubt not suiting her quite so well in others. So when the few advantages began to pall, perhaps in the daytime when there were no meals lying on the table and the benefits of the flat's central heating were a little less apparent, she might just pop along to Ardmory Road, and invite her good friend Warner to join her. What could be simpler? And – I'd seen the smile that she bestowed on him the moment I turned my back – what could be nicer?

And where did that leave Ian Laidlaw?

Nowhere, that's where. No more than *primus inter pares*, and only that if I pulled rank from being left with the privilege of feeding her. Otherwise, my standing was no higher than that of all her other casuals and cast-offs: the impotent and inconvenient, the tedious and troublesome, the spotty and stupid. I was no more than one in a line with all the unremarkable others.

It's hard to take, the loss of things so very precious. All my uniqueness? Bleeding away to nothing. Dignity and self-esteem? Lost irrecoverably. Control? *Control?* Walk through the barriers and you will find how much restraint lay in the bars, and how much in the creature behind them.

And I admit that now I wanted to hurt her. Desire to make her writhe and weep rose up in me, and when I shut my eyes against this seduction, worse pictures swam in front of me of Alicia squealing with fright and pain, Alicia beaten, Alicia bruised and shaken and silent. My clenched fists itched to punch her, my fingers to slap her pretty and complacent face, my body to pin her down good and hard and pay her out for all her sins and slights, real and imagined. My stomach knotted and my vision blurred. I clutched the body of the typewriter. Gripping its hard edges through the plastic cover, I let the spasm rip right through me, taking its time, robbing me of sight and hearing, tearing my insides, shredding me. Down in my trousers the pressure grew intolerable, like raw bruising. I nearly cried out with the pain. But though the sheer violence of feeling made me sweat, made me tremble, I admit welcoming it, and gladly, allowing it all the room it

119

needed to twist and thrive inside me, swelling and strengthening, fortifying itself. I not only let the adder writhe, I revelled in it. I encouraged it. Already somewhere, back of mind, I had a purpose; and though I'd no idea, still, what it was, this much I knew: to spite my sweet Alicia, I'd be a more than willing tool to serve it.

I don't know how long it was I sat there, how many minutes passed before the ringing in my ears began to lessen, the awful pictures to fade, my fingers to unstiffen. The typewriter cover slipped with a rustle to the floor, but I sat quite still, recovering myself, feeling my pulses settle and my anguish subside as the splinters of chaos around me resolved themselves once again into everyday objects. Things took their rightful places: well-labelled files on the shelves, neat stacks of stationery on top of the cupboards. The unruly rubber-bands lay quietly coiled in their clear plastic boxes, kept strictly segregated from the shining paperclips beside them. The pencils pointed upright in their jars, all sharpened ready against disorder. The quiet of the building slowly became my quiet. I felt more myself. Spreading my hands upon the desk top, prior to rising, I saw for the first time, lying on top of the files in the in-tray, that small, innocuous-looking slip of white paper there, and, on the dotted line, not the name we see now, Alicia's name, but that of someone else excused on the most unquestionable grounds – medical grounds – from attending all university classes.

How do these secretaries do it? I'd no idea a typewriter was such a complicated beast. It took a good ten minutes to find the little catch that lets the thing loose. And even when the roller was moving freely, I had enormous difficulty feeding the paper in and winding it up straight. I took my time practising aligning the type, and I experimented for some minutes with the correction fluid. Only when I was perfectly confident did I take up the small white slip and, drawing the little bottle closer, blot out with tiny brush strokes worthy of a Japanese artist, slowly, slowly, those nine letters in the name of poor, infectious Martha Anne Bowie which do not accord with letters in my Alicia's name. See for yourself, I did a good, neat job, a job of which, in execution at least, I could be proud. As for intentions, I'd nothing particular in mind. I think I'm being honest here. I think it fair to say that when I slid the plastic cover back over the typewriter, and tidied up the clutter on the desk, I had no more than a calm and general sense that all the time the little task had taken might, some time in the future, prove well worth the spending, that in some circumstances not yet apparent the little prize I slid into my pocket might come in very useful indeed.

Chapter 7

I felt quite merry, if the truth be told. On my walk home
across the park I made a point of quickening my pace in
order to draw abreast of Brown and offer to stand him a
pint at his local, but he said that it was Mrs Brown's com-
puter night, and I must excuse him. I felt quite regretful,
as I recall. I don't think I've ever really spent enough time
with my colleagues. Do you find the same? The acid of
administrative duty eats tiresomely away at one's day, and
there seems barely enough time to be civil, let alone
sociable. But, undeterred, I strolled along with him as far
as the wine shop on the corner of his street, and picked
up something a little bit special to have with supper. Not
that it crossed my mind for a moment Alicia would
notice. She may have been fettered with sensitivities of
which I was wholly unaware in the field of glues, say, or
mushrooms, or hallucinogenic weeds; but normally I

would as soon have thought of burning banknotes as sharing a nice wine with Alicia. It's just that I suddenly felt the need for a bit of a splash, an occasion. I felt like having a bit of a fling.

I bought our supper from the local grocer. It seemed a pity, after opening my wallet so wide for the wine, to turn all niggardly at the delicatessen counter, and I admit to making the sort of purchases I'd commonly eschew.

'Celebration?' the lady presiding over the till enquired.

'Of a fashion,' I said.

And to my mind it was, of course. Of a fashion.

The flat was all but dark when I let myself in. The thinnest line of light seeped out beneath the living-room door, but either Alicia failed to hear the sound of my key in the lock, or, still offended by my abrupt withdrawal at the end of the seminar, she chose not to come out and greet me. I carried the bags of groceries into the kitchen and, setting them on the table, got straight on with the task of preparing supper. I was a little surprised when Alicia failed to appear. Generally the rustle of foodstuffs being taken from their packaging, or the sound of a cork being pulled from a bottle, was more than sufficient to lure her promptly to my side in the kitchen. I was convinced that the sounds of a good meal well on its way would cause her to reappraise the very Spartan attractions of having a sulk; but when half an hour had gone by and there was still no sign of her, I became anxious. I'm not, by nature, a mean-spirited man. Dropping my chopping-knife on the board, I filled a second wine-glass and strolled along to seek Alicia out, thinking to soothe her ruffled feathers and then cajole her back with me into the kitchen with promises of even richer titbits than usual.

She didn't even look up as I entered. There she lay, outstretched on one of the more valuable of my rugs, crooning 'Kitty, kitty' in a most cloying fashion and dipping her fingers into a tin to offer them, clogged and discoloured with clots of offal, to Brightmony.

Showing the steady good sense that had accrued to him throughout a long life, Brightmony ignored her.

I stood in the doorway for several moments before Alicia had the courtesy to indicate that she'd become aware of my presence by lifting her face, if only momentarily, in my direction.

'There's definitely something wrong with him,' she told me. 'He just won't eat.'

Her voice was, I admit, a little unsteady. But the tears of other people are only water, and, under the provocation of seeing gobbets of cat food fall on a favourite rug, good intentions can drain away faster than sympathy gathers. I watched the slovenly tableau with mounting irritation.

'Possibly he prefers to have food in the kitchen,' I said. 'I might add that he wouldn't be the only one to harbour this somewhat antiquated prejudice.'

It took a moment for this to sink in, and when Alicia did reply there was an edge to her voice I'd not heard before.

'Oh, don't you worry! Brightmony's somewhat antiquated himself. If he gets sick, he'll more than likely die. That'll be good, won't it? You won't have the inconvenience of having him around!'

I regard heavy sarcasm as a kind of dialect for unfurnished minds, and was reminded once again of how very little Alicia and I had in common.

'Persist in that tone,' I warned, 'and I won't have the inconvenience of having you around, either!'

I turned and left the room. Promptly abandoning her listless cat, Alicia rose and followed. I might have wondered at this, given the flash of ill-feeling between us, had the reason not become almost at once apparent: continuation of hostilities. She waited till I had placed her wine-glass on the kitchen counter, and then, quite deliberately, she took up mine.

You don't think that's so heinous an act, do you? I saw the look that just crossed your face. You don't believe a little thing like picking up the wrong wine-glass amounts to a declaration of war. Come now, are you a married man, or aren't you? Let's have no cant. You know as well as I do that sane men and women have picked up carving-knives for less. The camel's back wasn't heaped high with boulders, you know, only straws; and Alicia was fully apprised from the day she moved in of my antipathy towards her own particular style of culinary collectivism, my disinclination to join her in regarding all spoons and dishes and teacups currently at large in the kitchen as mere joint stock. Picking up my glass was pure defiance.

But I had no wish to quarrel. Annexing the other, I placed it on the shelf behind, out of her reach. When I turned back I saw to my vexation that she had propped herself, with the most calculated lack of consideration, against the refrigerator door.

'Are you determined to provoke me?'

Her eyes widened. Alicia as *ingénue* was not a convincing spectacle. I moved towards the refrigerator and, wisely, she stepped aside, but as I delved inside the freezer compartment I saw out of the corner of my eye that she had taken the opportunity to reach over to the chopping-board and help herself to a generous fistful of my handiwork. Clearly, stuffing her cat with minced innards had slid down the table of Alicia's priorities. Baiting the hand that fed her had taken its place as the overriding objective.

I am no fool. I've had enough experience to know that when young people are set on battle, there's rarely any avoiding the upshot, whichever line one takes. And, sure enough, a moment later she was asking through a mouthful of sliced green pepper, 'What's eating you, then?'

Must I go on? You know the form. You surely don't need me to describe it. In your profession you must be only too well acquainted with all the semi-tones of practised insolence, the matching range of offensive smirks.

'Nothing is eating me, Alicia. You, on the other hand, are eating the ingredients of a supper I'm taking some trouble to prepare for us both.'

'Sorry.'

She didn't sound it. Not a bit of it.

She watched me lift the slivers of fish, one by one, over to the serving dish.

'Your hands are shaking.'

I laid the fish-slice down on the table.

'Take care, Alicia.'

'No, really. Look at your hands. They're shaking.'

I detest scenes. Fixing my eyes on the wall slightly above her head, I tried to quell the visceral stir by concentrating on taking breath. You wouldn't think something that comes more naturally than thought could suddenly prove a feat so awkward as to require almost superhuman control.

'Something *is* eating you. I can tell.'

An adder's eating me, I thought.

'What's the *matter*?'

I took the very greatest care not to answer.

'Oh, well. Suit yourself.'

She shrugged and turned, and would have walked straight out, had I not moved in front of her. What *is* it about women? A man who flounces seems ridiculous. We think him motivated by the shallowest pique, and barely worthy even of our disdain. He simply embarrasses. But let a woman flounce and she instantly maddens. We can discern no difference in the words, or their tone. But if a woman says them, she seems for just a moment to have allowed us to glimpse, through the shifting mists of her mood, the tip of a vast, hidden iceberg of disparagement, the floating tenth of a glacial underwater mountain of scorn. A man says, 'Oh, well. Suit yourself,' and our lips twitch with amusement. A woman says it and our fingers itch to wring her slim white neck and put paid to contempt for ever.

I'm not a strangler, so I hit her. I hit her very hard indeed. The blow I aimed was little short of savage, and, fortunately for both of us, seeing it coming she stepped back fast. None the less, my clenched fist came down on her cheekbone, hurting her badly and causing her to stumble. I caught and held her in my arms while she was still too shocked to cry, and when, to my relief, the weeping began, I took her by the arm and led her across the hall to the bedroom. I laid her down and pulled the cover over her because she was shivering. I closed the shutters and switched on the lamp. I fetched a bowl of tepid water to bathe her cheek, then flannels soaked in icy water, squeezing them out and holding them in place, praying the swelling I envisaged disfiguring her the next morning would thereby somehow be reduced. While she lay sobbing I sat beside her on the edge of the bed, carefully blotting the trickles of water from the compresses, stroking her arms and rubbing her cold fingers, anxious to comfort her in her discomfort and desperately hoping that somehow, amid all the concern and care and tenderness I showed, the absence of the one thing left unsaid might go unnoticed. But these words echo everywhere when they are not on the offender's lips. They rang in her ears as they rang in mine. These words go shrieking round the rafters until they're spoken, and I knew she'd hear nothing I might say to her till she'd heard them. And sure enough, soon enough, sick with the misery of waiting, she was reduced to begging me for the release they bring.

'Are you sorry?'

I'm not a liar, so I shook my head.

Her fingers stiffened in mine.

'You're not sorry?'

'I'm afraid not.'

The tears welled up all over again. It almost broke my heart to see them. I put an arm around her and, when she turned towards me for comfort, slid my free hand under her sweater and felt for the little buttons on her blouse. I pulled the layers of clothing off over her head and dropped them on the floor beside me. I peeled her socks off and tugged at her jeans. An imprint from them lay, a wide, red, ribbed weal, across her belly, making her look even more beaten, even more vulnerable. It was the last straw. Hooking my thumbs in the elastic of her underwear, I pulled the bright red patch of it, along with her jeans, off her body. I let my own clothing fall in a heap upon hers, and pulled her towards me, and though she would not stop her crying, she was acquiescent. I did not rape her. I am not that kind of man. But that night, for the first time ever, I made love to her just as I wanted, in my own way, in my own time. I made no attempt to please her or fall in with her body's predilections. For once I took her entirely for myself, to please myself, and in so doing allowed her first sight at another, darker side of me, a side always before kept very well hidden.

And she knew, too. And she accepted it. She knew what she was getting. And through all her shivering and tears, the involuntary stiffening of her body whenever what I did frightened her or caused her pain, the whimpers each time my hands pressed down on her poor damaged face, through all of this she was compliant. I am not telling you that she was passive, or obedient. I choose my words with care. I said compliant. I wanted her, yes, badly; but she was willing. I was brutal, yes; but she was still a partner. For all my fierce handling of her soft body, for all I took pleasures I could not have thought of before she somehow loosed this ugly side of me, I loved her. Were they such ugly pleasures? Well, who can say? What happens in a bed is private.

But not to you. For by the time the telephone on your desk rings, what happened in a bed is well on the way to becoming no more private than the date, or the weather. We must live in an ordered state and, by the rules, once you're involved in the telling, my right to privacy has been revoked. Well, fair enough. I am a conscientious citizen. I know how to abide by the rules. But I still have some claim to understanding, and your understanding is important to me. You sit your side of the table, I sit mine. I cannot fail to notice when you become uncomfortable, as you have now. I see the doubt that gathers behind your eyes. I know what you're thinking. Here, you are thinking, here comes the real cant. This man talks fluently enough, but he knows nothing. For all his shelves of books and sheaves of library cards, this man is worse than ignorant. He can look back upon his fierce demands and her weepy submission, and he can talk of love. You are disgusted, I can tell. With all the revulsion of a decent man, you think the lying has begun at last.

Not so. Not so. The time is coming, I'll admit, when I'll not be able to look you in the eye as we go on with this. But not yet. You must believe me, I knew Alicia's body as I know my own, and I say that, though there was snivelling and whimpering in the bed that night, there was pleasure too, and not just mine. Oh, yes, there was. Oh, yes, there was.

* * *

131

After?

After, I pushed her tear-streaked face away from me into the pillows because I couldn't bear to look at it. We lay in silence. From time to time her shoulders shook against mine with crying. My heart went out to her. Though it was late, and I was tired out, there was no question of my falling asleep. I lay with my arms around her till, driven with hunger, I had to roll away and, pulling on my crumpled shirt, go off in search of whatever might remain of our supper. It was thin pickings indeed. Everything I'd chopped or rinsed or peeled lay where it scattered when I hit Alicia, and Brightmony had recovered sufficient interest in life to have patted from the table on to the floor all the fish that he hadn't sampled. Sighing, I twisted the cork back into the wine-bottle and started on a trawl of the cupboards.

When I returned, Alicia's face was still buried in pillows; but from the heaving of her shoulders it was apparent she was crying again.

'Alicia, my sweet. Do stop, please. I beg you.'

Did she say something? It was so muffled as to be inaudible.

'What did you say?'

By leaning over her, it was just possible to make out the words.

'*Why* aren't you sorry?'

I sat beside her on the bed and took her hand. A wealth of things to say and no way to say them, except by telling her, 'Alicia, I'm rarely sorry for the things I do.'

Her fingers tightened round mine, but she said nothing. She must have realized, though, that things had

132

changed. She must have recognized violence for what it is, known that, just as the sharp, bright fragments of a child's kaleidoscope, suddenly shaken, fall in a different pattern, so everything between us had altered the very moment that I hit her. I was quite straight. I neither lied nor pretended regret. Is it my fault that Alicia didn't do what Margaret and almost every other woman would have done – set her bruised face with cold and ineradicable hostility, packed her belongings and left at once? Make no mistake, Alicia still had choices to make that night, and she was not in too much pain or confusion to make them, I am quite sure of that. Quite sure. I hurt Alicia deliberately, and she chose to stay. Am I to blame? No, I am not. And neither am I to be taken to task because, old enough to recognize the dangers that lie beneath such thin ice, I didn't throw her belongings into a bag for her, and order her back to Ardmory Road in a pre-paid taxi. Alicia was not a child. She was nineteen. Nineteen-year-olds habitually indulge in all sorts of dangerous pleasures. They race around on motorbikes, and drop from planes by parachute, and go down pot-holes. Nobody thinks of taking them into protective custody, or raising a storm against the middle-aged men and women who kindle the passions or furnish the equipment with which they choose to risk their young lives. And yet you look at me as though I were already culpable. Why? Isn't some bigotry operating here? Why should Alicia have to take her pleasures blunted? Simply because they were sexual? Come, that won't do. Put on one side all forms of cant – ancient and modern – and face one certain fact: what turns a person on is their own business. And if their

133

fortune is to fall in with someone who falls in with them, that is their business too. Am I to pasteurize my sex-life because to you it looks unsavoury? People can't hold off living out their stories for fear that it will end in tears. Most stories end in tears. Shall we get on?

Chapter 8

We had a sort of game, from that day on. Interrogation and intimidation were the nature of it. In that it had a name, I thought of it as 'Brightmony'. In that it had a purpose, it was to find out everything I could, and I began there.

'Tell you about Brightmony?'

'That's what I said, Alicia.'

'What about it?'

'Whatever you like, my sweet.'

'What for?'

'Let us just say I have decided to explore more fully the contours of your personality.'

'But why Brightmony?'

'It's where I've chosen to begin.'

She did her best. It was, in the beginning, a most disorderly exposition, a formless, trailing account of family members and pets and neighbours; of patrons of her parents' guest-house, entrenched rustic feuds, confusing agricultural practices; of shifting friendships and strange social rituals. I could make neither head nor tail of it to begin with, and had to feed her endless supplementary questions in order to clarify the simplest aspects of what, to her, seemed the least exceptional of events. It was like getting blood out of a stone. Sometimes I'd have to rise and dress and pace the room to stop myself from shaking her in sheer frustration at the snail's pace of the operation.

'What did you *do* inside this bus shelter, for God's sake?'

A long, long pause. You'd think it was the very first time she'd ever thought about these things.

'Well, we just sort of hung about.'

'"Just sort of hung about"?'

'Yes.'

'Talked?'

'Yes. No. I don't know. I suppose so.'

'Talked about what?'

'Nothing.'

'*Nothing?*'

'I don't remember.'

My fingers stretched out and tightened round the bottle on the mantelpiece.

'Really! I have forgotten what we talked about. Anything. Nothing.'

I'd pour myself another drink, small fortification for the next assault.

'Can I have one?'

136

'No. You've had quite enough already. Just carry on.'

Irritably, she'd gather the bedclothes even more tightly around her. I'd see her scowl reflected in the mirror.

'Well, it just so happens I can't think of anything else to tell you.'

'Alicia . . .'

'Oh, all right! Sometimes we'd smoke.'

Out it all came, painfully slowly. Evening after evening I pieced it together, this tale ineptly, inarticulately told, of growing up in such a one-eyed hole as Brightmony. Gradually I mastered the details of the lives of its inhabitants, fathomed its economy and worked out its social structure. I even learned its geographical perimeters, not as they appeared on the map, but as they were to her and to her friends, set more simply by the provenance or otherwise of all-weather footpaths or easy transport. Things that Alicia told me made no sense whatever, for example, until I worked out that Bellstane, twelve miles away by regular bus, was for her closer in winter than Cotty Hole, two and a half miles along a snowy and impassable gully; that Easter Blackwood, where the soldiers trained, might have been little more than a mile down the road so long as you kept your pretty face showing and your thumb stuck well out, and nowhere near the tedious fifteen the map might lead one to imagine. She talked, I listened, building the first shaky struts that were to form the cradle for growing understanding. Schoolfriends and pastimes, passions and prejudices, strange adolescent habits. Wherever possible, I believed what she told me, however implausible it sounded; and whenever what she told me beggared belief, I made a

137

point of at least appearing to give it credence. I would say nothing, but brood on it as though it were a small, annoying snag in my research work, bring it with me into the office in the morning, a nagging problem, and check out the possibility of its being the truth with one or another of the more approachable of my colleagues over the tea trolley. And on the whole this unofficial method of double-checking worked well. I was quite interested to learn how easily a desultory conversation about local government over the tea-cups may be steered round to some more unconventional topic without exciting anyone's attention. I had my moments of miscalculation. Brown took, I fancy, exception to my interrupting his dark mutterings on the subject of cuts in public transport funding to ask if either of his daughters ever 'just sort of hung about' in bus shelters. But once I'd referred in a moment of happy invention to the disquiet of a female acquaintance over her own offspring's choice of evening stamping grounds, he could not have been more co-operative – delivered me quite a lecture, in fact, on the topic of adolescent courting patterns in the context of local transport facilities. But I was disturbed to find how many of his observations left me as deeply in the dark as before. Lord knows, I never laid claim to an ordinary upbringing, but I had sadly underestimated my inexperience in these matters. To grow into manhood, as I think it's fair to say Brown did, with somewhat limited physical appeal, probably brings in its train all sorts of virtues of augmented sensibility born of the absence of brash confidence. To grow up totally within the forbidding cocoon of ugliness like mine brings with it no such compensations. Ignorance and awkwardness were my best friends. I never 'just sort of hung about' a bus shelter in my life.

So evening by evening I listened to Alicia's ramblings, mastering new ways of looking at a world I'd never known and she'd grown out of. It was strange territory, and I had to be ever vigilant to try to see it as she had, through clear eyes set in an unspoiled countenance, and judge it accordingly. I must say it seems to me that she'd had jam on it right from the start. Born to a caring couple who'd longed for children for years and been delayed by problems of a gynaecological nature, she was adored from her conception. And in so far as I could make out, the arrival eighteen months later of baby sister Rowan contributed no more than a general feeling of relief and added contentment throughout the household. Probe as I might – and did – Alicia's bitterest day appeared to be the one on which her younger sister learned to ride her brand-new birthday bike before Alicia herself mastered the art. The sharpest words she could remember hearing from her mother stemmed from some trivial rosebush-stripping incident. Her father didn't seem to have sharp words in him. The proud parents showed their daughters off to everyone, and after the family moved down the road to take over the guest-house, the two girls soon learned to show themselves off. Smothered with affection and larded with compliments from comfortable summer visitors, Alicia padded down the lane to nursery school. No trauma there. She made two friends on the first morning, and both remained devoted, bar the odd transitory spat, through primary into secondary schooling. Here she can hardly be said to have gone through the wringer, having been taught every subject in a manner that struck this listener as, to say the very least, not overly taxing. Nothing and nobody frustrated her. Her sister considerately grew an inch taller, and lent her clothes. Her mother's sheer thankfulness for maternal urges brought to successful fruition persisted through the years. Her father mended her punctures promptly and taught her to fish. She was even permitted to hang up her violin and ballet shoes as soon as it was clear to everyone she hated both and had no talent. She kissed her first boy on the cheek at twelve, dabbled considerably more deeply from fourteen onwards, and lost what tatters still remained of her virginity to some blond and bony hitchhiker from Wisconsin who had the good fortune to pass through Brightmony the night before her sixteenth birthday. She didn't even have a hard time here, it seems, since her period co-operatively began the next morning, and her distaste for his apparently quite normal – not to say generous – male sexual organs sent her scurrying back to the chaste safety of books for what turned out to be a crucial year, academically speaking. By seventeen she had both overcome her initial repugnance for the physical characteristics of stark-naked males, and sat her Highers. She'd even popped into a Brook clinic while visiting her auntie in Aberdeen. From then on, it was party-time.

It's hardly a chronicle of sorrow and adversity, is it? She had her gripes, but I must say that they were none of them calculated to tug successfully at this man's heartstrings. I tried to see her point of view but, frankly, the more I listened to Alicia's ramblings, the more I realized with disconcerting flashes of bitterness how very much her childhood differed from mine. There were small areas of coincidence, of course. I too could recall with painful vividness the old frustrating sets of temporal limitations – school times, bus times, meal times, bed times. I could remember what it meant to think in terms of freedoms hemmed arbitrarily by family rulings, to judge diversions not so much by their intrinsic attraction as by their sheer availability.

'I didn't know you smoked.'

'There's not much else to do, somewhere like Brightmony.'

'Who bought the cigarettes?'

'Depended.'

'Upon what, Alicia?'

'On who had any money, of course.'

Another laborious detour, to prise out the pecuniary details. It made some sorry listening, to be sure, this tale of pocket-money whittled almost to nothing by fines or loss or prodigality. Occasional earnings might speed the cash flow. More often, miserable funds would be augmented in less admirable ways, by petty theft or a more imaginative disposal of school lunch money than parents reckoned on, or by what I came to think of as Brightmony disease – self-induced bouts of amnesia with regard to the handing back of small change after errands. This was a weakness from which Alicia, I'd noticed to my cost, still suffered; but on the whole it was another world, this Brightmony. The more I learned, the more I wanted to find out. Until I listened to her telling me, I hadn't known a normal childhood.

'Kissed you?'

'Well, yes.'

'Inside the bus shelter?'

'Only sometimes. Only a bit.'

'A bit?'

'Well, not a lot.'

'How much? How? Show me.'

'*Show* you?'

'Yes, show me.'

I'd pull her out of bed, onto her feet.

'This is the bus shelter wall, right? So, show me.'

She'd stand in sullen, lumpish refusal, until I started pushing her backwards. The gathering heat of the radiator against her bare buttocks took on the force of argument, and in the end she was compelled to show me or burn.

'Thank you, my sweet.'

So we progressed, little by little. I learned all sorts of things. I learned about her father's bitter and unremitting warfare with the moles in his front lawn, her mother's passion for fruit-growing, even the intimate details of her sister's erratic menstrual cycle. (Erratic, that is, until resourceful Sister Alicia dragged Rowan, too, to visit Auntie and others in Aberdeen.) I know more than I care to know about Rowan's relationship with a sergeant called Malcolm from Easter Blackwood. I know the sisters' musical preferences from the year dot, the colours each dyed her hair to annoy their father, their school high-jump records. I know the portions of Rowan's anatomy Alicia coveted, and those she didn't. I learned how boyfriends can, between close sisters, be swapped back and forth almost at will like cheese labels or postage stamps. I learned the reason why I didn't get a phone call on New Year's Eve (though since I am assured that for the most part it concerns Rowan's misdemeanours rather than Alicia's, I shan't divulge it) and how to decode Brightmony slang. I learned the difference between this drug and that, and the precise import of several dirty words I'd never even heard before. It all took time, though even that was unpredictable. One evening she'd be nothing short of recalcitrant; the next, unnervingly compliant. But even during our easier and more agreeable sessions I might catch her in a little holding back, a barely perceptible protective pause, as she attempted to preserve some tiny island of her privacy.

'What were you going to say?'

'Nothing.'

'You were about to say something. You thought better of it. What was it? I want to know.'

'Nothing. Really.'

'Alicia, you know that I don't want to have to force you.'

'It wasn't anything, honestly.'

'Honestly' is a giveaway. Have you found that? The moment she used that word, I'd always know that she was lying.

'Tell me.'

I'd take her wrist between my hands and twist the skin in both directions, making her squeal.

'You're hurting me!'

'I mean to.'

'You'll break my wrist!'

'I doubt it, sweet. I think that you'll have told me long before that.'

'All right. All *right*!'

And she would tell. More often than not I'd have to hide my smile of incredulity and amusement at what she'd thought to bother to hide. I'd be amazed that she should have so misplaced a view of my opinion of her that she could hesitate to tell me such things, presumably for fear that I would think the worse of her. What did she think I thought, for heaven's sake? I'd hear the sordid little tales of fumblings in the dark under the bridge with local boys, and petty sexual experimentation with summer visitors. They were no more than I expected. I'd wipe away her freshly rolling tears of humiliation, cheer her along with gentle raillery and, when she'd finished, take her in my arms all the same.

And slowly, slowly, she became better at telling. Or maybe I asked better questions. Interrogation is a skill, like any other, as I'm sure you'd be the first to agree. Not that I'm giving you much opportunity to demonstrate your own proficiency. Few of your clients can have my facility for confession. I must be money for old rope for you. Alicia, now, would have held out rather better, I assure you. She'd plead a headache, loss of memory, or desperate tiredness. She would distract, or irritate, or play dumb. She'd set out, mid-way, to seduce instead, and finally you'd have to pin her down or take a handful of her hair, give her a savage slap or two, to keep her talking.

'Go on.'

'I'm tired out!'

'I said, go on.'

And with a sullen shrug, and one of her formidable scowls, she would begin again, somewhere else if I let her get away with it, on the same topic as before if I were firm. And then I'd stroke her fingers, and warm her chilly toes for her between my thighs, and pass her little slabs of chocolate, one by one, to keep her going and reward her. Gradually her peevishness would dissipate, her voice would settle and her limbs relax, and we'd be off again.

And slowly, slowly, I became better at listening. So when she spoke of bus fare misspent, and walking all the way home from Drummournie, I'd shut my tired eyes against the lamp's glare, the better to hear the whole sorry tale, and find myself beside her under dripping trees. As she kept talking under my steady, patient prompting, I'd feel the raw cold of the mist on my face and see it hang in palls over each stunted wind-warped tree, shrouding each drystone dyke and lonely sheep-fold. Her voice led on, over grey rocks and scattered stones, over bare hills and marshes, and it was just as though I walked with her, through eerily quiescent farm-yards; along the fringes of dark, sodden woods where water spurted at every footfall; up the rough cart-roads with twin streams running down the wheeltrack beds; up, up, past lichen-plated birches, up and up, to where the only living things to see through mist and drizzle were black-faced sheep, the only sounds above the whine of wind, sheep calling and the work whistle of a far-off man to his dog. Then, 'Ravens,' she'd say. At once I seemed to see a pair of them corkscrewing in the thick, grey sky. Or 'Deer'. I'd see their hard, dark crotties lying on cores of snowdrifts. 'There was a hare.' And there was one for me, materializing no more densely than a ghost in the weak light, but there none the less, as though at her command. She'd speak of scrambling up the next steep slope and I would see it clearly in my mind's eye, leading up into the gloom of an oak wood and, farther along, bare scarps of rock showing like sore places on the crest of the ridge. She would fall silent and I'd take my time, letting the picture I held in my head fill in and focus, the colours deepen, before I'd increase the pressure of my hand on her, to spur her on to further efforts. 'Some of the gullies still held patches of snow.' I felt the crunch of it beneath my feet. 'Some of the tarns had swollen into waterfalls.' My ears filled with the rush of water, tumbling and creaming over great rocks. My face stung with the ice-burn of spray. Until I lay beside Alicia and listened to her telling me, I hadn't truly known the country in winter.

'Go on.'

'It's nearly twelve!'

'Go on, Alicia.'

And she went on. 'Sometimes we'd go along the river.' Along the very river whose loops and curves I'd sat so often tracing on the map with my fingertips as though they were my own scars? 'There's a small path goes down beside the bridge . . .'

I'd listen carefully, and gradually I was beside her once again, feeling it too, the ground here giving under my feet with soft squelchings, there giving me the spongy lift of moss floor, as though the denseness of the gravity in this place she talked about could alter without reason or warning. The country is a strange place in the dark, and

146

even with Alicia for a guide it's foreign country to a man like me who hasn't trodden on earth in years or, if he has, has barely noticed. It might have been another planet she was talking about, it felt so odd. Springboards of sponge change imperceptibly into a treacherous suction. Disorderly bushes slap the intruder wetly in the face. Random drippings surround him. I am a man accustomed to straight paths of concrete under my feet, and when I reach out it is to touch the unyielding security of brick, the perfect dependability of glass, or planed wood. This place she talked of was a giant wet jungle, and it exhausted me.

'Is that enough?'

'Yes. That's enough. I am worn out.'

'You! *You're* worn out? You're only listening!'

Only listening, indeed! There was so much I wanted to know, I wore myself beyond exhaustion to find it out, but she didn't notice. It's fully twelve miles over the hills between Brightmony and Drummournie, but when I let her stop she wriggled like a puppy freed from the leash, and within moments of my rolling my weary body across the bed away from hers her indefatigable young fingers were scrabbling the short distance over the sheet to where I lay, weak from this gruelling addition to the exertions of a long working day. She'd set about provoking me to further physical efforts, running her tongue over the contours of my face, puckered to even deeper runnels than usual by spasms of fatigue, and she would think no more than that I was kindly making a face to please and excite her. Never tell me Alicia loved me. If you don't see what's in the other person's eyes, then you're not loving;

and I tell you Alicia Davie never looked at me except to get from my sheer hideousness that little extra sexual charge that kept her willing in my bed. She couldn't claim, as you or others might, that she was deterred for reasons of susceptibility to what was on view. She, of all people, could have looked. She should have looked. Mangled my face may be; it does, for God's sake, bear some expression. You can see weakness in it, exhaustion, distress. She only had to turn her eyes. But no. Except in so far as she could glean her own aberrant gratification from what she saw, she was indifferent. Alicia could gaze, purely for her own pleasure, at my poor face, and she'd not notice it was grey with weariness. She can't be blamed. With everyone hanging admiringly over her cradle since birth, watching her face to make sure she was content, how should she ever have started to learn to watch theirs? To her, tics of fatigue in the eyelid and bloodless skin were, like thinned lips and frosty silences, an alien language of which she'd never even learned the alphabet. These things washed over her like foreign babblings on an ill-tuned radio. Indifference gives pain to any lover; but to an older man it brings with it an even richer humiliation. Life is a strenuous business, after all. It tires one out. Why would one drag one's body through all those weary, grinding years simply to be ignored or overlooked? What kind of grand finale is that?

Alicia aged me, that is the fact of the matter. Believe me, it is a nonsense that young lovers enliven. It was Alicia Davie who made me feel old. Before I knew her, I never worried about my health or strength or endurance. I never had to. I never feigned sleep, either, pretending insensibility to probing fingers and wishful caresses, desperate to husband flagging potency through one more night. You couldn't call Alicia a sensitive lover. She was far too demanding, far too selfish, and when, from spite, she put her mind to it, a regular little detumescent, to boot. It wasn't easy, I assure you. Disparity in age brings in its train a thousand other small disparities, and some not so small. She'd scoff at my quaint habit of keeping a saucer under my tea-cup, and I could smile. I'd see a quirk of speech of mine catch her attention, and though I knew that she regarded me as a linguistic fossil, something chipped from a former age of speech, I was not ruffled or offended. But strength's another matter. There are no small disparities in that. Kept wakeful through the early hours by aching limbs or pounding heart, I'd run my hand across her soft, fresh, sleeping body, cushioned by unlived decades from all the weaknesses and saggings of mine, and such a feeling of sadness was raised in me as I could hardly bear. Other times, too, I'd catch her eyes on me as I eased into welcoming bathwater or sat hunched at my desk after supper, and know at once what she was thinking. I could pretend I hadn't noticed, but things seen cannot simply be sloughed off like grubby shirts. I'd feel her gaze on me and straighten up, pull in my belly muscles, move with a quickened purpose. But it was always a glance too late. I had been told by her again, without a word spoken, that she was young and I am old. I am no wishful thinker. I can face facts. Each time I came home to an empty flat, each time I stepped out of the secretaries' office and saw her giggling in some doorway with Warner, I knew that I was closer to the day she packed her tatty belongings in a bag and stuffed her cat into a cardboard box and took herself permanently back to Ardmory Road, to younger and more vigorous pleasures. I couldn't hope to keep her through love. She was too young to have a heart. But, then, I'm too old to let the things I want slip through my fingers without a fight. And still – no, more than ever – I wanted her.

Chapter 9

What for? What *for*? What kind of question is that, for God's sake? What for, indeed! She was what men my age reputedly dream of, wasn't she? A soft and nubile partner, willing to muss the bed, retaining the child's capacity to make heartlessness pardonable and ignorance charming. Why shouldn't I be desperate to keep her?

Silence. You sit quite still, the absence of expression on your face proof of your incredulity. And you're quite right. Disingenuity is not my style, and you have asked the best of questions. What for, indeed?

She had become for me, you understand, a road back. In her insensitivity and mediocrity, her negligible qualities of soul, lay something I needed, something to which, now she had inadvertently awakened me, I desperately wanted access. She held redemption in her gift. In her unremarkable childhood, her commonplace youth, there lay some clue to what was missing in mine, and I was bent on going back to search for it. Now you could argue this was mad, and were it any other man's life under discussion, I would agree with you. If this were just another seminar, I'd whip in without hesitation, 'Laidlaw here thinks he can go back and find whatever was ripped out of him by next door's dog on that, his fifth and last happy birthday. Does that make any sense to the rest of us? Suppose a man born black in white society broke off his living to go in search of some fair-skinned version of himself? Suppose a woman took it into her head she might have been a man, and went to find him? Ridiculous, I think we'd all agree?' And I'd be right. Pursue that line of thought, and all of us might sit around for ever, pointing reproachful fingers at Fortune.

But I'd be wrong. For ugliness like mine is something special. It's not just a choice of fewer pathways: it's a choke-chain and iron post. It's not a matter of soaring only on prevailing winds: it's clipped wings and a permanent grounding. I told you, I rank myself along with the grossly deformed, the helplessly crippled. Don't expect me to look across the room at amiable, uncaring Alicia the day she starts to pack her things and simply shrug my shoulders, lend her a suitcase, and say, '*Tant pis.*' Listen, I watched her flirt with Warner in my seminars, his virile assets more and more manifest each time the tediousness of the topic in hand provoked fresh thrashings of his long, cramped legs; and from the look on both their faces as I ran through the principal components of Gaullism for the third time (and purely for MacFaddyen's benefit) it was quite evident Ardmory Road would see that pair of busy visitors again before too long. I'm not a selfish or possessive man. She could have Warner, he could have her. But only hole-and-corner, as it was now, and taking hardly any of her time, until I'd finished with her, until she'd told me everything, until in knowing Alicia inside out I'd learned exactly what I'd missed and what sort of person I too might have been. Is that too much to ask? Is it? I'd housed her, fed her, pleased her and kept her warm all winter. She could stay long enough to finish one little job for me, surely? It was a small enough thing. Just tying up the loose ends of a little piece of research work, that's all. I realize that to you, with your face, it probably all seems a very silly matter. To me, with mine, it seemed one last proffered opportunity for self-understanding, a strange, rare gift well worth the getting hold of. How often does a man like me get to feel he's being offered a glimpse into the other side of things, the way the others live and think and feel? I told you, for me the world's been filled with rocks, not people. Cool, courteous, un-assailable rocks. To get inside Alicia was, in some sense, a little experiment for my own satisfaction – like prising apart a toy to peep at the clockwork, or cracking a bird's egg to prod the unborn soft stuff inside. It was to this end that I'd been probing Alicia deeper and deeper, coming to know, as they say so facetiously about my own line of work, more and more about less and less. I didn't even envisage its taking more than a couple of weeks to finish the job. Three at the most. And then, if I were strictly honest with myself, a large part of me, most of me, was desperately looking forward to being rid of her. Yes. Rid of the burden of her once and for all. It would be both a joy and a relief to be free of the constant hovering of embarrassment, the growing sense of guilt at having so totally withdrawn from all the wider responsibilities of a job like mine. It would be good to get some work done at weekends, to eat in tranquillity, to sleep in peace. I longed to be able to hear my own doorbell ring and not cringe inwardly for fear some passing colleague had taken it into his head to drop in. In all my years of living here, it hasn't been a frequent occurrence. I keep myself to myself, and people respect that. But it has happened, and in my mind's eye I saw it happening over and over. I'd imagine my visitor sidling, despite my lack of any real welcome, past me into the hallway. I'd hear him remark appreciatively on the flat's spacious Georgian proportions, step forward for a better look and, glancing idly through a doorway, catch sight of my sloppy little nestmate sprawled on the floor in front of the television set with all her sleazy, tell-tale aura of intimacy and permanence. I'd watch him putting two and two together. I'd see myself curdling with shame.

Oh, I'd be glad enough to see her go. Getting rid of Alicia, shipping her back to Ardmory Road, was a pleasure I promised myself when I was done, a well-earned reward for a task well completed. But till then I wanted her with me. I'm not a dabbler by nature. When I start something I like to finish it, if only out of habit, for thoroughness' sake. It is a characteristic of my profession (though not, alas, one shared by too high a proportion of my own colleagues), this willingness to hang on and root out the last of things, keep searching until conviction comes that there is nothing of significance left to be learned. And things would keep on coming to light, though in the most tangential fashion.

'Shared the *tub*? With your *girlfriends*?' (Lord knows how we got on to this.)

She wriggled her back beneath my fingernails.

'Don't be a prude. Down a bit.'

'A prude? Me?'

I ran my fingernails down quite a lot, to prove this was no prude scratching her back. The skin glowed pink where I was gently ravaging. She squirmed under my hand, forever easy to please with a man's fingers.

'Sharing a bath is nothing. You only get to look. After school hockey we used to share showers.' She rumbled with contentment, like a puppy. 'Left now. Left. *My* left.'

My fingernails wandered left. She drew breath and her soft bottom clenched.

'Cold showers, or hot?'

'Christ! Hot, of course! You wouldn't catch girls in a cold shower, even if they were plastered in muck!'

'I shall remember this freshly revealed female antipathy, my sweet.'

'Up a bit. More.'

Up a bit. More. My obedient fingers crept up and over her shoulder. Promptly she squawked and brushed them off.

'If somebody scratches me there, I—'

I rolled her over.

'Not sure I care for this "somebody", Alicia . . .'

As usual, her struggles lasted only as long as I allowed them. But something she'd said stuck in my mind, and all that evening and the next day I felt it pushing at the stiff door of memory: *if they were plastered in muck . . . plastered in muck . . . muck . . .* The phrase crept in my brain all through the departmental seminar, distracting me horribly from Brown's dissertation, entitled, to the perceptible detriment of seminar attendance, *State Autonomy under Advanced Capitalism: A Statist Analysis of Central State Penetration of Municipalities.* All very worthy stuff, as I assured Brown as warmly as I could bring myself to do straight after – but it didn't make the most gripping address, and I sat through it stiff with discomfort, impaled on my jagged splinter of memory: *plastered in muck . . . muck . . . plastered . . .*

After the seminar, I walked to the nearest chemist, that large one on the main road that seems to specialize in army-sized bottles of shampoo and acne lotions. What do the students do with all the stuff they buy? Do they drink it? It's clear from looking at their skin and hair that either the products are criminally ineffective or most of them cannot read the instructions. I strolled up and down the aisles for quite a long time, certainly long enough to draw the professional attention of any undercover floor-walkers. I still had no idea what I was searching for, but it was coming. It was coming.

Pots. Pretty pots. Pretty, flowered china pots and small, dark, glass bottles and oddly shaped plastic vials and sensible-looking aluminium tubes. All colours, shapes and sizes. All prices, from fairly steep to downright outrageous. I prowled and peered. I took the tops off one or two, and sniffed. I even smeared globs from a couple into my palm. You'd never think there were so many colours for faces and mouths and eyes and fingernails. Why don't they come to my lectures looking a little bit brighter? Once I got started picking and choosing, it took no time at all to gather what I was after.

If I were to tell you how much I was asked to pay for a few half-ounces of contemporary woad, those eyebrows of yours would whip up like greyhound starting-gates, and you would murmur incredulously, 'Still no idea . . . ?'

But still no real idea of what I was after, although the tiny packages rolled out of their thin plastic bag and up and down the dark floor of my briefcase, so I was made uncomfortably aware of their presence on every step of the walk home. By the time I reached the flat it had been dark for quite a while. Alicia was in my dressing-gown, the lazy slut, floating about waiting for me to hang up my overcoat and start on her supper.

I unpacked my goodies and set them out on the table. Apart from an offhand 'I hope it's not fish', Alicia took no interest at all in my purchases. She didn't give them so much as a glance. She simply gathered up the newspaper I'd brought home with me and drifted off towards the door, rooting through for the television page.

Quickly, before she left the room, I started up, 'How was the seminar, Ian? Well, thank you for asking. I can't say that I was carried away by intellectual excitement, except in some rather small particulars; but I do think a few trenchant observations on the topic of regional water-rates were made in the discussion that followed.'

She'd turned in the doorway. It wasn't at all like me to attempt to attract her attention.

'If you were to press for detail,' I kept on, 'I think I'd

be forced to admit that Jones's contribution, as usual, was little more than right-wing political opinion masquerading as sober academic thought; but Stuart McFarlane broke with habit sufficiently to open his mouth, and one of the graduate students offered a few ill-chosen words on—'

I broke off. She had come closer, and was pointing.

'What's that lot, then?'

There was a fairly lengthy pause. And then I told her.

'Those are for you.'

She stared.

'I don't wear that stuff on my face.'

She was quite right. In all the time that she'd been in my house, I'd never seen her daub herself with anything except my under-arm deodorant and that black stuff some women rub around their eyes. And Margaret didn't put make-up on her skin, either. Most women do. Do you think it was pure coincidence that neither of the females in my life ever put goo and powder on their faces? I don't. I think it was no more coincidence than my left-handed dentist. These things run deep.

'You're wearing this stuff on your face tonight.'

'Oh, yes?'

'Yes.'

'Why?'

'Because I say so.'

'I *hate* that stuff.'

I wasn't to be thwarted. Pulling her over towards me, I slapped her bottom hard through the thin fabric of my dressing-gown.

'Dear heart,' I said, 'each day I shop, each night I cook,

and every morning I bring a steaming cup of tea to your bedside. Now do one small, sweet thing for me, will you?'

I tipped all the little bottles and packages into the capacious dressing-gown pocket. Holding her firmly by the elbow, I steered her, clinking gently, into the bedroom. I lifted the mirror down from the wall and propped it on the chest of drawers to lean against the wall, catching the light. I dragged a chair across the room, and put a pillow on the seat for comfort. I pushed her down on it.

'There. Off you go. Make up your face.'

She glared at me in the mirror.

'What's up?' she asked with spite. 'Missing Margaret?'

I gave her the evil eye.

'One more word, poppet, and I'll slit your throat.'

I settled comfortably on the bed, watching. Reluctantly, she dipped her hand into my dressing-gown pocket and drew the contents out one by one, wrinkling her nose with disgust as she peered at the labels and dropping what packaging there was provocatively onto the floor. She lined up my little gifties, and considered. Then she reached up and pushed her hair back from her face, running her fingers through it. She looked quite different then: older, and rather curiously so. But I'd no interest in that right then.

She picked up a squat opaque bottle and shook it hard. Unscrewing the top, she put her middle finger over the hole. She tipped the bottle over and back, fast, and dabbed her finger on her cheek. She did this several times, dabbing a different part of her face each time, till she was covered in leprous beige patches. Then she put down the bottle and, for the first time, lifted her eyes to herself in the mirror.

And it came back. Slowly, slowly, and I at first unsure of its validity, but it came back as I had known it would the moment I slid my hand in my back pocket to check on my wallet and stepped across the road to the chemist. I watched her smear the viscous, peachy muck over her cheeks, out to her hairline, into the delicate runnels around the wings of her nose and up, up across her forehead, around her chin and down in smooth broad strokes into her neck, and suddenly I found the skin on my chest and shoulders and upper arms twitching, crawling, afire. My nose and ears filled in that suffocating underwater way. My mouth went dry, my vision blurred, and I could feel myself squirming and shrieking and slapping out and fighting, and feel my mother's heavy, stockinged knee pinning my chest down on her double bed, and smell the strange and sickly smell – violets, for God's sake! Violets! I've loathed the smell of violets all my life! – as her thick fingers rubbed the foul muck into my still tender scar patch, plastered the sore side of my face with it, spreading it thickly and unevenly because I was struggling hard and she was angry, and both of us knew from the moment her eyes fell on the bottle on her dressing-table and she reached out for it, that what she was doing was never going to work.

'Get it off! Get it *off*! *Get that muck off my face!*'

'Stop *struggling*, Ian! Keep *still*! Do you *want* to go around looking so hideous?'

What do the scientists say? That every syllable we utter must leave its imprint on the universe eternally? Hideous.

That's what she called me. Hideous. I was a *child*. I had four good, strong limbs, and skin as cool as china, and deft little fingers. I had a mop of curls, neat ears, fine brains, straight eyes. Can't you be loved once you've been flawed? Can't people even look at you and smile any more?

My mother was ashamed of me. Deeply ashamed. Forget neighbours with dogs, there were to be no more neighbours at all, she saw to that. She found a house built by a misanthrope, and inasmuch as a boy's life can be reduced to fields around his home and the few miles of road that led to school, mine was. Believe this, if you can: after that accident I lived so isolated a life, was kept so close, that but for the blessed Scottish Education Acts they might have built a tower and locked their hideous little changeling away inside, and had done. All family friends were dropped. Relatives were avoided. I can look back and count upon the fingers of one hand the few who were permitted inside that house. I see my mother shivering on the doorstep, her nose whipped rabbit pink by wind, wiping her chilled fingers on her apron. Would she invite whoever it was she was speaking to over the doorstep and out of winter's grasp? No, she would not. For then I might be seen more clearly, and the brief look of commiseration above my head might drive her nearly mad, for she now lived out all her days stretched so tight on a rack of self-pity that one small screw turn of another's sympathy could prove disastrous. All social situations were shunned – not so obviously as to give rise to speculation or to offence, but still shunned. It was a subtle process that was set in train by the plopping on our

161

doormat of any invitation. I see my mother now, thin-lipped with misgiving, picking up a blade to slit the length of fancy envelope as if she had a throat in mind, easing out first the gilt card, then the greased lie, 'A wedding! That *will* be nice . . .'

And then had to be acted out each painful particular of some six weeks of farce. There was the sacrifice of time and money on a new suit for me, expenditure all the more bitter because the suit to be replaced still hung in a dark corner of the wardrobe, outgrown, itself unworn. There were the hateful, poking fingers of her intrusion, gathering in sham intensity as each day passed. '*Won't* it be fun?' 'It *will* be nice for you to play with all your cousins again after so long!' 'You *must* remember Auntie Marjorie – you used to *adore* her!' And as the day of celebration finally crawled round the last week's corner, there came the bitter moment of my father's forced collusion with her decision born of prescience. 'Don't buy the travel tickets yet, George. Just in case . . .'

Just in case? Just in case, on some glorious June morning – the sort of morning, no doubt, on which Alicia's family piled off to weddings in great good spirits – my mother should rise early from her bed after a sleepless night, and, coming to mine, lay her hot palm across the cool, ploughed skin of my forehead and whisper, 'I'm sure he's a little feverish, George. Perhaps we shouldn't think of going after all . . .'

Through a feigned flutter of lashes I'd see his face fall. Why, though? Could it be that he was slower than his own child to recognize the way things were? He's dead now, my father. I can't go stamping on his grave demanding, 'Were you *really* that dense?' He was what people call 'a gentle man' – far, far too gentle to ease my mother aside for long enough to lay his own hand on my forehead and hazard the Plain Man's Diagnosis, 'He seems all right to me. Why don't we chance it?' Let others call that gentle. I call it weak. It was my face, for heaven's sake. If I were brave enough to run the gauntlet of covert stares and silent sympathy, then so should she have been. And he should not have pandered to her cowardly evasions, or played his servile part in all her cheap contrivances to such perfection.

'Good thing I never bought those travel tickets!'

Good thing? Good *thing*? The scorchings of disappointment will, in the end, burn out a child's hope. I'd bury my ever-spoiled and ever-spoiling face deeper in pillows so I'd not have to hear her rattling yet another unworn suit away out of sight in the wardrobe, or listen to her steady, complacent humming as curtains fell on this particular charade, so well performed, so very satisfactorily ended. Bunched under suffocating blankets, determined out of sheer cussedness to take prolonged advantage of the privacy and peace to which my 'fever' now entitled me, I'd take myself alone to the promised occasion – a drowsy pillow-pilgrimage of wayward trains and scrambled timetables, of negligent guards and spinning clock hands. I'd arrive late, but not so late I missed my heart's desire, my eternal daydream: the sour, untidy, gifted Edinburgh surgeon who drew me almost roughly into the harsh shaft of light from a window and said, with all the brusqueness permissible in the superbly skilled, 'Ha'e ye no proper doctors in the borders? What ha'e they all been about, leavin' a laddie to look like *this*?'

I shared my daydream with no-one. There were to be no brothers, no sisters. (One disappointment is enough.) I had no friends. No-one was ever invited to my house for tea, and though I was dutifully asked to birthday parties from pity, I had no close companion in school, no-one to jostle with in the playground. The young are brutally fastidious, and all the moral chivvying in the world is worthless the moment the preceptor strolls round the corner. But there were compensations. Where did the bookishness begin if not at home and school, keeping my face safe out of sight behind hard covers? Swift. academic progress earned great respect, and even a little human contact. 'I dinnae ken. I wasnae listening. Ye'll have tae ask Ian.'

Lonely I may have been. I'm not aware that I was unhappy. I was a quiet lad. I slept and ate and rode to school and back, and ate and slept. I made no fuss and caused no trouble – indeed, it would never have occurred to me to do either. And such was the headway made that at the age of twelve I found myself transferred alone to yet another school and cycling twenty-seven miles a day in pursuance of my fine education.

This is a stretch of life I now remember as clearly as if it were filmed, so free is it from all the strains and passions, the moods and manias that make a turbulent blur of other people's histories. I passed these years in little more than growing more informed, and taller and stronger, until the masters let me be, and twenty-seven miles of cycling became more of a pleasure missed at weekends than a fatigue to be dreaded on Monday morning. Odd, though. I rode that journey season in and season out for six whole years, but it was lost to me until Alicia talked of Brightmony and stirred up memory. Then I could shut my eyes and see it roll before me again, the fields and hills pale and still under a winter sky, the trees wrinkled with cold, the sheep rooted in rime. Along the edge of burns the only sign of life came from cold, flashing sparkles of sun on water clear as gin. The countryside was hard, impregnable. The bike was part of me. Wind whipped my face into horrifically mottled colours, and the attack on each steep incline added a working grimace. Downhill the bike winged, and the grimace turned into a grin of triumph. I tell you, the sight of me spinning, a livid horror, round some tight corner has scared more than one faint-hearted tourist into a border ditch.

That bike was my life. I even cycled to Oxford and back on that bike each term. I was the first to go on from my school to an Oxford college; but like the rest of my not inconsiderable achievements, it was viewed by the rest of the world more as a gift given than a gift earned. That's one of the more curious things about stigmata. They set a man apart in more ways than he might imagine. Once a man has so clearly tangled with Fate that the marks show, and show so terribly, he has to others a heroic air and nothing about him from then on is his own. It is assumed that there are still gods watching over him, breathing down his scarred neck as it were, granting him this boon here in tardy compensation for past sufferings, denying him that boon there out of continuing spite. And people like to play at being gods, and make amends where it is in their power. This has advantages. It's certainly the explanation for my inordinately generous scholarship; and it's probably the reason for my early and distinguished promotion. (I like to think that, anyway. Given the dismal standard of most professorial appointments in British universities today, I'd hate to think I'd been selected by the same criteria.)

So there you are. What I remember could have been a good deal worse. I'm not a man to snivel on about a rotten childhood. I wasn't beaten, starved or ridiculed. I had three meals a day and all the books that could be furnished me. A man can't crab at that – at least, I won't. I must say I despise the modern tendency to look back at beginnings and rattle chains. Look back by all means. The farther one moves into middle age, the more it interests one to lift the sheets on one's inception. Self-pity is another matter entirely. I'll not be part of that. I'll sit and watch Alicia smearing that vile muck all over her face because I ordered her, and I'll recall some trivial incident mislaid. But when it finally comes back, when I've remembered, it's just the slotting of another small, flat piece into the jigsaw of my past life. That's all it is. It's not a reason, or an explanation, or a cause. It doesn't even form a part of some great lofty excuse or justification. It's just a little memory, a scrap to be filed under 'not forgotten after all' before I indifferently turn back to my reading.

'How's *that*?'

It was more of a cry of satisfaction than a query. I looked up from my books. She'd swivelled on the chair so I could see her clearly. Not only had she done something quite extraordinary to make her face look glossy and inflexible, like a doll's, but she'd also puffed up her hair in rather the same way as the lady with the blue rinse in the delicatessen.

'You look repellent.'

'I do, don't I?'

She seemed delighted, grinning all over. Her eyes looked like prunes in a stale yellow pudding. Her puffed hair wobbled on her head. I was disgusted.

'Please wipe it off.'

Her face fell.

'Can't I just keep it on for a bit? It took *for ever*.'

'I'd much prefer you to remove it.'

'Oh, all *right*.'

A steady stream of clattering and sighing left me in no doubt whatever that getting the stuff off was neither as pleasurable nor as successful as applying it had been. There was much muttering about the absence of 'cold' cream. I tried not to let her distract me; but by the time she scraped the chair legs back viciously over the polished floor to let me know that she considered she'd finished, I'd lost the thread of what I was reading entirely.

She plopped beside me on the bed.

'What was all that about, then?'

'Never you mind.'

'Not going to tell?'

'Certainly not.'

'I looked like Margaret, didn't I?'

'Not in the slightest.'

She'd let the dressing-gown fall open. Its glossy red cord lay over her bare belly like a fresh weal. I felt like whipping her, and maybe I should have indulged my instincts instead of persisting in vain attempts to read.

Now she was craning her neck over my shoulder to see the title of my offprint.

'*Corporate Strategy and European Industrial Policies*. What on earth are you reading that for?'

'Up until now I've been permitted to read what I choose in my own home.'

'Touchy, touchy.'

I raised a hand in menace and she rolled away, scraping her back against the pile of volumes I'd massed beside the pillows.

'Ouch!'

'Do be quiet.'

'That really *hurt*.'

Her attempts to reach the sore part of her back and rub it were making the bed shake. I was exasperated beyond description.

'Do you want to find a bed without books, Alicia? I'm sure that there are plenty about the town.'

She broke off rubbing. Her face shone, leftover grease and malevolence combined in roughly equal proportions.

'I bet there are,' she said, very nastily indeed. 'I can think of one straight off that has something in it a lot more exciting than any of your books.'

Well, well. A little threat. A little warning. I'm not an eyebrow-raiser like you on the whole – since I only really have one to raise, the gesture lacks some of its customary punch – but I admit to watching with some alertness as she flounced round the room, gathering up a matted hairbrush here, a lump of dank towelling there, on her way to the bathroom and a good, long, wet sulk. This wouldn't do. This wouldn't do at all. Time enough for all-change when I was ready, not her. Warner could wait. He might be wanting her for one thing, and I for quite another, but like him I had discreetly under wraps the wherewithal to achieve my ends. He might have all the allure of youth and a bed without books, but I'd learned an awful lot about Alicia. And to get what he wants, if only he wants it badly enough, even a man like me may, when hard-pressed, stoop to a little expedient makeshift and cunning.

Chapter 10

Makeshift and cunning. To keep Alicia with me that little bit longer I had to strengthen my hold in some way. What better method than pleasing her more? It's not my style, but I can stretch a point once in a while. The longer I thought about it, the more sense it made. And so to learn about what pleased Alicia, I, on the side, embarked upon what I conceived, in that I thought about its parameters at all, as a fairly limited programme of sexual investigation. Limited! I see you smile. More know Tom Fool than Tom Fool knows, and, yes, you're right, I'd made the serious mistake of failing entirely to take my own nature into account. I am in every way a meticulous man, and I soon found that what began as no more than an attempt temporarily to bolster my own position flourished and grew into a hideously demanding enterprise in which there was no longer any room for all the vagaries and distractions of my own passion. I, who had thought I knew her body backwards, started casually again, this time with her body only in mind, and found that, to give it even for a moment my undivided attention, I had to stamp on all physical impulse, crush all self-interest, keep my own body firmly under control. But I persisted. I had no choice. Before I knew it, it had become a challenge. I quite deliberately turned myself into a pleasure-giving machine, and applied myself to monitoring Alicia's responses with the same thoroughness I would accord any task: gathering the information, double-checking each little inconsistency, testing out hypotheses, consolidating every small gain. You know as well as I that any endeavour holds its own interest. The more exacting the undertaking, the richer the rewards it brings. Soon I was taking quiet pride in my new skills, enjoying plotting tiny advances, relishing their attainment, deriving, in short, enormous satisfaction from learning to screw out of Alicia's senses all the raw, squealing possibilities of gratification.

There's one indubitable advantage of self-curbed passion. You get to watch. With all the superiority of the professional survey over mere amateur susceptibility, your estimation of the effect you're having shifts from a series of sexually blurred impressions to clinically sound evaluation. The spilling ragbag of surmise is traded for orderly assessment. If I do this, that happens. If I do that, this. Faces and bodies may try to lie, but if you get to watch you can see flushes crawling over skin, sweat sheeting, muscles pulling taut. No need to slide a finger in warm, damp places to feel some hidden pulse go throbbing. You've seen it already, if you were paying attention, here in the crook of her arm, in her groin, under the shadow of her jaw. Certainty nourishes skill. Skill becomes palpable. Is this how self-protecting virgins prick-tease so horribly successfully?

And incontrovertibly, as though to prove the efficacy of the scientific approach, Alicia's capacity for taking pleasure from me grew daily. It was, I now realized, less what I did to her than how I did it. There was a way of handling her, speaking to her even, that had an effect little short of mesmeric, rendering her almost entirely unresisting, and putting her in some strange, quiescent frame of mind where everything about her stilled except the delicious, biddable senses.

'Give me your hand.'

I'd wrap the end of one of Warner's useful little lengths of rope around her wrist.

'And the other.'

She'd watch impassively while I twisted and knotted, threading ends neatly around the struts of the bed-frame and out of sight, sliding a finger between her skin and the finished knots to make sure they weren't too tight for her comfort. Her eyes rolled up, not in the mock exasperation of the tractable partner amiably co-operating for the other's delight, but with the full surrender of the entirely spell-bound as well as bound. Alicia's sexual preferences were obvious. The firmer I was with her, the more responsive she became and, to my great relief, concomitant with her snowballing excitements, I found my own residual desires melting away. This, in turn, made the process far more efficient. By dint of careful, steady control often over hours, necessitating all my concentration and patience – by dint, too, of never allowing Alicia to slip over the brink into exhausted, inarticulate satisfaction until I myself was fully satisfied – I gradually winkled out of her the sorry secrets of a dozen affairs, everything, what this one said, how that one's body felt, why she left Tom for Mike and, later, Mike for Tom again. I showed no leniency. I was implacable. Sometimes I kept her up half the night, rousing her back to wakefulness over and over, tormenting her with my demands, making her reconstruct entire quarrels, forcing her to resurrect long-forgotten pleasures, describe them to me in the greatest detail, codify and rank them. I pried in the most intimate places, grilled her on the most private of things. Sometimes she'd balk, but then the care I took would win her over once again. My carefully calculated provocations would prove irresistible. My sweet compulsions would defeat her. It was a game, after all, and one which her occasional recalcitrance only prolonged and heightened. Alicia enjoyed it. She liked my power over her. She had no comprehension whatsoever of what I was after. Self-bound to the extent of having no real insight into others, she took no interest at all in my intentions. She simply gave herself over again and again to my control of her body, submitting herself with pleasure to pleasures to which Margaret, forever fettered by a sterile sense of her own self-esteem, would only ever yield safe in the private lock-up of fantasy. There are two ways of being sexually bound: Margaret's and Alicia's. You come to your judgement; I've come to mine. I am a liberal man and, as such, I stand for personal autonomy. I've had both women in my bed and know the one for whom, in this respect at least, I formed the deepest admiration.

But in this respect only. In almost every other I found Alicia a tawdry creature. The human infant takes close to twenty years to develop the talents, fill up the mind, and achieve the maturity considered pretty well essential for life on the planet. I think it would be safe to argue that, bar her considerable sexual skills, all that Alicia had to show for herself could have been tucked under her belt in a quarter the time. What of her parents and her teachers? Weren't they all mortified, filled with inexpiable shame? How had they come to let her grow to have no intellectual passion, no moral fervour, no ambition, no imagination, no fire? Alicia, I can assure you, was what we call 'average'. Indeed, if you consider that this is a university, we have to say that she was better than average, far better. And yet, show her a Titian and she'd remark upon the dust on its frame. Let her catch sight of Bertrand Russell in some television documentary, she'd make a comment about his hairstyle. Spreadeagle her across a bed and ask a million questions about former lovers, she wouldn't even wonder why. Not for the first time in my life, I found myself consciously grateful I'm not a parent. I would not choose to bear the awful responsibility of having fathered a girl like Alicia. A nation gets the government it deserves. The children, too. I'm glad that I won't be around to see this little lot achieving high office.

And so the nights went by whilst I refined my skills, ransacking her body the more efficiently to ransack her mind. She wriggled and squirmed. Pleasure heaped high on pleasure for Alicia as I demanded the answer to question after question, a seemingly never-ending process as each answer raised its hydra head of dozens of further questions: questions to clarify, to illuminate, to check. It took its toll. Alicia might sleep all day, but I still had a department to run, secretaries to placate, students to organize. I need my sleep. Fatigue makes me waspish. I could be filled with irritation by the mere sight of her body sprawled in luxurious insensibility across my bed when I dragged myself home, drawn and exhausted, from another long day fast on the heels of another long night.

And sometimes, under the pressure of this irritation, I went too far. I twice duped her by insisting, through all her desperate denials, that she herself had in some other long-forgotten context already admitted to things I firmly supposed to be true. Both times, in the end, she broke down and confessed. And once, wholly unforgivably, I even tormented a promise out of her, redeemed under supervision immediately after, to fetch from Ardmory Road all her personal letters. I read them through at my desk while she slept. It was a dispiriting body of correspondence, I must say: ill-written, studded with all the embarrassing pretensions of youth, riddled with mawkish sentiment. When I had finished, I laid it down with a shudder, relieved beyond measure that no-one has ever sent letters like that to me.

But nothing, not even shame and disgust at my own behaviour, could stop me. I wouldn't let up. I kept on at it, determined both from obsession and the sheer force of professional habit to finish the job, root out the last of it, assure myself once and for all that I'd missed nothing.

Can you find yourself through another person? Of course you can't. The very notion is ridiculous. Any account of self amounts to no more than a blurred and shuffled pack of lies, and, as for interpretation, modern psychology is scarcely less crude a tool than any of its equally tedious forebears – augury, crystal-gazing, palmistry, cards. Except at the bare level of facile prediction, one can know no-one else and there's more, even to oneself, than one thinks. And yet I claim I learned about myself through her. Indeed I did. Clues came to light, but more, I found, through my manner of questioning her than through her answers. I learned that I did not relish power over another. That I'm not tyrannical by nature. That I'm not one to take my pleasure in drawing blood or breaking bones, and in so far as a sadistic man may only express true tenderness where he gives pain, I am no sadist. Listen, one day I left her bound, just for a moment, to slip down and buy fresh milk for coffee – for hers, you understand, not mine; I take mine black – and the moment I stepped back inside the flat I knew she had somehow worked herself free. Where was the steady fizz of my straining kettle? The demented lid-rattle of its final achievement? Clearly she'd simply wriggled from her bonds and padded through to turn the gas off. But was I irritated? Not at all. It didn't spoil my pleasure to walk into the bedroom and see her there, propped up so comfortably against the pillows flicking through some back copy of *The Listener*, licking the sugary biscuit crumbs from her fingers. She looked for all the world like some much-loved wife waiting for one more morning cup of tea; and though I tossed the papers down on the bed, and warned her, 'Next time, my precious, I shall use chains,' I felt no more, no less, than a moment before. Her helplessness had not aroused me. Her little outburst of autonomy did not repel. I'm a grown man and have no need to take my pleasure from domination. If I stood over her and threatened to scorch her swollen little nipples with drips of candle wax, if I wrapped Warner's chains in a tea-towel and chilled them thoroughly in the freezer before I laid them on her belly, it was to make my bedfellow a sight more biddable, and not myself a bit more tumescent. Alicia's squeals may have amused me; her tears, thank God, did not excite.

Indeed, little about Alicia now excited me, just as little of what she confessed excited attention. Most of what she was telling me tied in with topics she'd already covered, a good deal of the rest I could predict, and the details bored me. Oh, I kept at it none the less; but little of interest gradually turned into less, and less turned into almost nothing and it was very clear to me that from my point of view, at least, the game of Brightmony was drawing inexorably towards its close. Alicia would miss it, though; that was for sure. I've never seen a body, even in films, laze in such attitudes of happy satiety. I've never seen complacency spread quite so richly over a face. But she was young and the young are resilient. She'd all the time in the world to teach young Warner to please her as I did. Given that her pleasure sprang from what I did to her, and how, and not in any way from my being who I am, that shouldn't give rise to any real difficulties. So long as Warner was a keen enough apprentice and had, as one might say, all the right tackle, he could learn how to do the job. He might even suit her better in the long run. He was younger and fitter, and though he didn't have my striking looks, he probably had an adequate equivalent: that strange capacity more common in the young for taking sex depersonalized in much the same way as people my age take tea without sugar.

And that would go down well. For Alicia, it must be said, was no love-maker. She was no sharer. Indeed, over the time we'd been together she'd even made it clear that she regarded my rather old-fashioned prejudice in favour of mutual and synchronized orgasm as some poor, petrified leftover of juvenile ambition which she, with fuller experience, had quite outgrown. Sex was, for her, a private and limited business. Orgasm was not a matter for wonder, an impetus to reflection or self-assessment, a manifestation of deep or lasting feeling. It was a charge, a thrill, mere jangling of ganglions. She brought nothing to it except her most willing body, and she took nothing away. However many times we might come together, she was the same girl after as before. Essentially, she was a masturbator who went to bed with me because it so happened that my particular assets and touch made the charge greater. But only because it so happened. And, had it not, she would have slept alone and played with herself, or gone out looking for another. I couldn't ever claim, as a man who is loved can, that my touch was all the sweeter for being mine. I furnished a rather special face, a slightly menacing tone of voice and the occasional good hard slap to which she responded, much in the same way as a piece of battery-operated equipment ordered by catalogue and sent by mail under plain cover might furnish equally dependable service to somebody else. In Alicia's ingenious form of auto-eroticism I played no more of a part than the ropes or the straps I provided, and was expected to have no more feelings than those limp, lifeless objects brushed away after. Sometimes I wanted to take her by the shoulders and shake her. 'This is *me*. This is *me*, Alicia. Not just an ugly face!' But she would not have recognized the parody, let alone understood the heartsickness behind the cry. Reared in the most effective of fetters – knowing no better – she was impregnable. She offered little, and I could offer little in return.

Are there a lot like her, do you suppose? It's an appalling notion, too awful to dwell on, great armies of them all getting older and yet incapable of reaching however belatedly, some form of true maturity. They're mutually sustaining qualities, ignorance and insensibility. Ignorance comes first. We'll pay for offering them these educational short-commons, these tedious years of thin school gruel in which we floated only a few bland lumps of information and sentiment. Look at the damage. Put on one side their awful ignorance of history, of cultures, of man's ideas – all the sheer breath-taking wealth of what they don't know. All that could at a pinch be made up. But ignorance atrophies growth and growth won't wait. That can't be made up later. There are no second chances at life. Look down your list of local evening classes. You just won't find it there, *Transfiguring Adolescence (Advanced)*, waiting until they're quite ready to take it.

So what's left to these products of a model childhood, for whom knowledge has been diluted beyond its power to nourish, and sex introduced without its terrors, guilts and darknesses? Look at Alicia. A mind impoverished, and sex become an empty game. It might as well be Space Invaders she was playing at, for all her intimate encounters induced her to develop or left her changed. Sex never caused Alicia to feel sad or thoughtful, disaffected or despairing. It simply 'worked' or 'didn't work'. Credit where credit's due, she'd done her best. To try to liven up this drab inheritance, she had invited Horror in to play, and he'd brought Danger. But it was all still play. I'd strap her up against the bars of the bed-head, and even before the first buckle tightened around her wrist, she'd be complaining.

'That *pinches*, Ian.'

I'd take her other wrist, and reach down for a second strap.

'You surely don't suppose that I should loosen it, simply because you say it hurts?'

She did, though. It was a game to her, that's all. But my face is not a mask I can slip off the moment her bodily excitements have shuddered to a halt. I *am* a horror. I live behind this face day in, day out, and her insensitivity continued to rile me. Not that I was the only one to suffer. Brown complained regularly over the tea trolley about her extremely irritating assumption that he was always happy to lay down his own work at a moment's notice to pick up hers. The spotty philosophy graduate in the wheelchair was still waiting after weeks for the date that she'd promised him because she was simply too lazy and thoughtless to make her position clear at the outset; and poor Rowan languished through a compulsory term in France, loathing the country and everyone in it, without receiving so much as a sisterly postcard in return for her persistent flood of miserable letters.

She was equally unthinking about everything else. Her views on public issues smacked of the gutter press. Her attitude towards other races and cultures was condescending where it fell short of being downright offensive. And as for what she said about her abortion – oh, nothing to do with me, I assure you. All that was over months before I happened on the scene. But little things she'd said had made me suspicious, and in the end I managed to winkle the pitiful little story out of her. And though the details themselves are of absolutely no interest – the inexplicable combination of inept delays and truly chilling efficiencies must be entirely common to this sort of small, routine, surgical procedure – her attitude towards the business, quite frankly, shocked me. She didn't express red-blooded and rational relief that she had been relieved at no financial cost to herself of some inconveniently expanding clump of insentient cells. She didn't look back on the grisly occasion as the little killing it was, and feel either irretrievably wicked or sensibly realistic. She didn't even feel what might in the circumstances have been understandable – a little perverted self-admiration. She simply went pale and rubbed her forehead with her fingertips and stammered through her tears some sentimental drivel about how having the baby 'might have been so nice . . .'

Oh, she was hopeless. I leaned against the mantelpiece and watched her snivelling at the recollection I'd forced and I came to the firm and final conclusion that, if

Alicia's upbringing was typical, I'd missed a lot but I'd missed nothing. And there was little I could say or do to improve her character or whittle away at her inadequacies. Advice takes the shape of the vessel you pour it into, and Alicia was no different from all the rest of her age-group in proving to be impervious to suggestion. Besides, their deficiencies are not my problem. By the time they reach me it's all far, far too late. And I'm getting older all the time. I'm tired. I do what I am paid for conscientiously, but I can't be expected to spend my very limited free time sorting out a bottomless pit of Alicias. I'd had the one, and she alone had proved more than enough.

I wanted her out. The fire that was my passion had burned itself out, and in its place lay only ashes of preternatural calm. The days were crawling past, but I knew that sooner or later I'd have to make some sort of move. One evening I let her stay watching the television while I went off and did some work. The next night I left her wallowing until all hours in the bath. The evening after that she watched the television again. Alicia herself said nothing about this sudden change in the set pattern of our existence. Indeed, I said nothing about it myself. But that Sunday, waking late, I opened my still weary eyes to see the harsh rods of morning sunlight falling across her bare buttocks, and, feeling absolutely nothing, told myself almost out loud and with a depth of relief quite indistinguishable from sheer joy, that it was finished. I had no interest in her at all. Exposed entirely, both in body and in mind, she left me utterly unmoved, completely indifferent. With all the certainty of the experienced torturer who rolls the bloodied body over with the tip of his boot and knows there was nothing to be learned after all, I realized the whole appalling business was quite, quite over. I was a free man once again.

Chapter 11

Or could be soon, once I was rid of her. Do problems stretch, like time itself, to the end? My eyes fell on Brightmony, nesting on one of several heaps of her crumpled clothing washed up against the walls of my room. The smell of cat was in my pillows. Alicia's leg lay over mine. I ached for order to lay my eyes on, for quiet to work in, for peace of mind. But how to get her out? How do you ask a woman to leave after so many weeks of sharing a bed and a bath and a table? I wanted her to go, quickly, no fuss, no scenes – that very day, if at all possible. Out with her mangy pet and such finality that there would be no question of her ever materializing on my doorstep again. No wistful looks across the room in seminars. No notes marked 'Personal' lying on my desk or in my pigeon-hole. No telephone calls. No regrets. No reminders. Just me free in my former self, and Alicia tucked in her own squalid bedding with Warner, relieved as I to have the whole affair safely behind her. To get her out, and at the same time scupper any temptation on her part to apprise Warner, or anyone else for that matter, of the sordid nature of our relations. There you go, raising those eyebrows of yours. No easy enterprise, you're thinking.

No? No? Come, the solution's pretty obvious, surely. A simple matter of pushing Alicia just that bit farther, beyond the enhancement of sexual excitement, and over the edge. It's easy to outrage a masochist. They're very sensitive indeed to anything that they perceive as an affront to dignity. They don't spend all that time flirting with shame and self-abasement for nothing. All that I had to do was go too far. Nothing too difficult in that, surely, bar the small obstacle of my natural reluctance to implement so distasteful a procedure. All it would take to clear my flat of her and her effects for ever was the deliberate contrivance of Alicia's humiliation. Make no mistake, I am not talking now of kiss-the-rod games. Forget the gentle intensities of sexual submissiveness, the unaccountable seduction of physical surrender. I'm talking of humiliation, and of humiliation so intense that it would not only cause the instant and total annihilation of intimacy, but also furnish the useful little legacy of searingly unacceptable memory, that ineradicable saboteur of any future desire to tell tales. What did it matter if she spent a few days holed up alone in Ardmory Road, sobbing her eyes out? It didn't. I'm not so mean I wouldn't compromise myself a little to help her out. It was no trouble to me to make the effort to come in to work sufficiently early to introduce the little white slip from the Health Centre into the unsorted pile in the in-tray. That would, effectively, cover her absence in the unlikely event of Brown suddenly going on the rampage.

I am a patient man. I take my time. I waited, lying peaceably at her side, until she woke and stretched and uttered her usual grunt or two of what I had always sup-posed to be matutinal greeting. I waited as she pulled my woollen dressing-gown out of shape round her shoulders and slouched her way, half-naked, out of the bedroom. I waited until I heard the bathroom door close. Then I sprang into action. Reaching down under the bed to where the necessary hardware lay, I hauled it up beside me and started to slip the best of young Warner's chains around the sturdy struts of the bed-head in careful, closely thought-out preparation.

I heard the lavatory flush before I was ready. Alicia rarely paused to rinse her hands. She padded straight back in and laughed to see me kneeling naked on the bed still slotting the little metal catches in place.

'Oh, God! Not again! I haven't even had my breakfast!'

'Shan't either, sweet. Work to be done.'

I reached out, fast, and caught her unprepared. Holding her tightly by the wrists, I pulled her down beside me on the bed.

She struggled, still a bit sleepy, irritable.

'Lay off! I don't feel like it. Let me go!'

I slapped her hard – 'Lie *still*!' – and pushed her flat, my knee pinning her down. She fought for breath as I worked with a speed and skill born of long practice, pinning her firmly in place, no slack this time, no cautious testing of the tension, no thought for tender skin of wrists or ankles.

'What are you *playing* at?'

'Be quiet, Alicia.'

I sat back on my heels, satisfying myself that she couldn't move an inch. I'd stretched her out in the most inelegant fashion and she, aware of this, was tense and hostile, embarrassed even.

I took a good, long, steady look at her, and colour flooded her face, neck and ears.

'Ian!'

I slapped her again, and further patches of red rose under my hand. Now she was really close to tears.

'Ian! Take them off, *please*! They're *hurting*.'

'I asked you to be quiet, Alicia.'

I took my time, dressing. Enjoyed the leisurely tranquillity of sliding a fresh shirt from its hanger in the wardrobe, discarding one pair of shoes for another, selecting a tie. Brightmony stared, unblinking, from his vantage-point on the window-ledge. I stared as coolly back at him. Then I walked out without a backward glance at either of them, shut the door, and breakfasted alone, listening to the peal of local church bells with more than customary appreciation. Soon, once again, things will be this restful, I comforted myself. Very soon. And so pleasant was this field of reflection that it was only after a second cup of coffee that I could bring myself to return to the bedroom.

She twisted her head away sharply as I came in.

'Sulking, my sweet? I'll leave you to it.'

I closed the door on an obscenity, and went into the

188

study to write some letters. When I came back, over an hour later, she turned her head my way but was barely more civil.

'What do you want to know? Tell me! Be fair!'

I sat beside her on the bed. She was a sorry sight, I must say. Filthy mascara tear-tracks ran down both sides of her face and disappeared beneath her hairline. Her body was all chilled and pasty-looking. Even the skin round her nipples had puckered into goose-pimples.

I ran a finger down her belly, considering. I was aware that this was a last chance I threw away here; but no, there wasn't a thing I wanted to know.

'Nothing.'

I could tell at once that she didn't believe me. Women are so vain.

'It's Allan, isn't it?'

'Allan?'

'Allan Warner. You think that he and I—'

I put my mouth down hard on hers. I'd no desire to hear her views on what I thought about the one small pocket of her existence she was so vainly and pathetically still trying to keep to herself. But let her not believe that she and young Allan had secrets from me. Moving my mouth across her cheek, I whispered in her ear, 'These chains, you know, are borrowed from Warner.'

'I don't believe you!'

Clear that she did, though, for it shook her into silence. And I took advantage of the hiatus in the conversation to reach down beside me for *The Times Higher Educational Supplement* and unfold it protectively in front of my face. The quiet snivelling that began after a moment or two didn't disturb me overmuch. After a while I stopped hearing it, really.

Men of my age attach some value to their comfort. I loosened my tie, eased off my shoes, and, leaning against a pile of pillows – both hers and mine – I worked my way gradually down the pile of reading matter that had collected beside the bed. This is a normal Sunday practice for me. I like to keep up with the periodicals. Some of the articles in foreign newspapers are germane to my particular research interests. There are some columnists in the weeklies I particularly enjoy.

It was some time before Alicia disturbed me again.

'Ian! Ian! I can't feel my toes!'

Without removing my eyes from the newsprint, I eased the lump of Brightmony off her ankle with my foot. I soon regretted my compassion for within moments she was complaining loudly, wriggling and squirming as much as the tight chains allowed, agonized by the needles and pins of returning sensation.

'For pity's sake, Alicia! I'm trying to read!'

'You shitty bastard! Let me go!'

I have no patience with this kind of language. These days one hears it from students only too often. I slapped her again, and this time considerably harder than before. For once she didn't fall to snivelling, but seemed, on the contrary, sufficiently defeated to lie still and quiet whilst I skimmed through a couple of longish book reviews in *The Times Literary Supplement*, though out of the corner of my eye I could still see the muscles in her calves tightening over and over as she surreptitiously tested her strength against that of the chains. I couldn't help but smile a little. This stuff's seen Warner across the Cairngorms.

I might have known the peace couldn't last.

'Ian! I have to go.'

Lowering an issue of *Political Quarterly* to which I'd just transferred my attention, I looked down at her enquiringly.

'Go?'

She blushed – rather becomingly, I thought. I'd never realized that she had a modest side.

'Please, Ian . . .'

'Let you go? You mean, to the bathroom?'

'Please . . .'

'No.'

I went back to *Political Quarterly*. I'd run my eyes over no more than a paragraph or two before: 'Ian! I really need to pee!'

'Oh, for God's sake, Alicia!'

Hurling my reading matter onto the floor, I wrenched my tie taut under my collar, and reached under the bed for my shoes.

'Ian! Where are you going?'

Both eyes and voice were filled with alarm. Brightmony, immobile on the pillows, stared at me balefully.

'Out.'

'Out?' She lifted her head in panic. Her hair was matted, sticking in streaks to tear-stained cheeks. 'You can't just leave me here like this!'

'No?'

'No! It's far too dangerous! Suppose . . .' She broke off

unsure even what to begin to suppose. I stared down at her, filled with irritation. What sort of trouble, for heaven's sake, could she suppose that she might get into, shackled so firmly?

'Suppose there was a fire!'

'A fire?'

I couldn't help but be amused. The poor thing seemed in quite a state.

'Now how would a fire start, Alicia?' I knelt on the bed and reached across her. 'Somebody being careless with matches?'

There, on the bookshelf, a little box of them lay next to the candle.

'No, Ian! No!'

The rasp of striking match seemed to fill her with terror. She shut her eyes tight, like a child.

I held the small flame up in front of her.

'Look, little Alicia. Open your eyes.'

She acted deaf and kept them shut.

'Don't keep me waiting! Open your eyes!'

Still no response. The match burned down so far that it warmed my fingers. I shook it out and lit another. I held this one so close that she could feel the heat from it moving down slowly over her belly. She flinched, more, I am sure, from fear than from discomfort. She caught her breath. Her whole body stiffened.

'Ian—'

'My sweet?'

Lighting a third match, I took a little tuft of pubic hair between my fingers and held the flame near till the thatch of it sizzled and melted into tiny worm-droppings.

Tendrils of fine grey smoke curled in the air. The smell of scorching rose between us. I watched tears force their way between her eyelids, track down her grubby face and disappear.

She turned her head away from me, and I stood up.

'I'm still intent on stepping out for a while. Do you still wish to raise objections?'

She shook her head, her eyes still tightly closed.

'That's better.'

I left the bedroom door ajar so she could hear, clearly, the sound of the front door closing behind me, my key double-locking it carefully, my footsteps taking their time down the stone staircase. I pushed the heavy main door open, enjoying the first invigorating lungfuls of air. It was a cold and beautiful morning.

My Sunday papers are not delivered to my door, like the dailies. I fetch them myself from the Pakistani grocer around the corner, and since he's the only shopkeeper in the street to open, there's often quite a line of people waiting their turn between the crates of vegetables and the freezers. For once I didn't mind. It took a bit of time for me to calm down, standing there waiting behind all the others, unable for some moments to rid myself of the disquieting picture of Alicia held so very vividly in my mind's eye. And no-one else had any idea – not Grubby Green Jacket just in front of me, craning his neck to weigh the rival attractions of Sunday papers; not Tall and Unshaven, shovelling the last of the croissants into a bag; nor Fatty, reaching up for more cornflakes. It suddenly struck me, as I looked round at each of them in turn, that any or all of these unprepossessing people might, just like me, have someone waiting, someone who strained to hear the trifling, unremarkable sounds of their returning footsteps, someone spreadeagled unwillingly and indelicately over a bed, ugly with tears and desperation. It was a sobering thought. But then, as daily papers keep reminding us, there's more goes on in the world than we think. For all we know, half of the queues we stand in are made up of sadists or murderers or madmen. There's plenty of them about. They must shop somewhere.

The line inched forward at a snail's pace. Perhaps I should be willing it slower. Was it possible Alicia hadn't caught on yet? She was, as I have stressed, insensitive to a degree, but God forbid that I might go to all this trouble and she still manage to persuade herself that this was no more than an unaccustomedly savage and sudden tightening of – if you'll forgive the crude but unintended *double entendre* – familiar screws. Even Alicia couldn't be that dense! She couldn't, surely, be laid out so uncomfortably up there kidding herself that with my return, and the confession on her part of some lame tale featuring herself and Warner, the world would come to rights again, and I'd reach gently over her as usual, releasing her with sweet words and soft kisses, and offering all the little favours she'd come to expect after my small brutalities, the milky and comforting coffee, the chocolate rewards, and, after I'd taken the empty cup from her hand and laid her down again among the pillows, my ever more skilful physical solace for all her pains? Oh, surely not! Impossible! She *must* have grasped the point. It *must* have worked. Everyone has a snapping-point, for God's sake. I must have pushed her up to hers. Surely I'd climb those stairs and set her free, and with all the ashen courtesy of the ineffably hostile she'd step around me, purposefully never once meeting my eyes with hers, just staying long enough to pick up from the floor sufficient of her garments to get her home, pulling them on, adjusting them at wrists and ankles to hide the raw, round marks of my abuse from curious eyes. Surely she'd scoop up her cat and walk out on me with all the determination of a Margaret. This awful scheme could not miscarry. I'd thought it out. It had to work. I'd planned to be a free man, and I'd be one. Flattening myself politely against the freezer to let Grubby Green Jacket past, I forced the dreary fear of failure out of mind, and stepped up to face the waiting shopkeeper.

He was, contrary to habit, civil. As he turned to snarl instead, at his wife, toiling too slowly in the dark recess of the small shop matching supplements to papers, I felt my spirits lift and optimism slowly returning. Of course things would work out as planned. How could they fail? In less than an hour Alicia would be gone. I'd gather up all her remains, everything, down to the last unpartnered sock, the last squeezed tube of herbal handcream, and send it after her in a taxi. I'd spend the day vacuuming cat's hairs from my rugs, laundering bed linen, wiping Alicia's sticky fingerprints off the refrigerator door. At supper time I'd open a nice bottle of wine, perhaps look up a concert on the radio, put a whole packet of the olives she detested into the salad. Things would come out all right – indeed, already were coming out right. In paying for milk and papers (no chocolate today: no need for chocolate now) I successfully emptied my pockets of cumbersome change, and as I stepped out of the shop the sun sailed from behind the clouds, warming my face. There was even an abandoned dustbin on the street corner in which to drop the colour supplements. So flawless suddenly seemed the world, and so exhilarating the certain prospect of peace ahead, that I was only momentarily taken aback to feel the unwonted spring in my step, and realize the whistling on the stairs was my own.

It's three flights to the top. Generally I take them at a steady old pace, but on this occasion, fired with such unaccustomed good spirits, I took them almost at a run, and every reason to thank Providence after, for there on the very top landing, his fingers already on my bell-pull, his head just turning at the sound of my approach, who but Brown?

I was appalled. Simply appalled.

My poor heart banged. The whistle died, mid-trill, on my lips, and even the sudden silence echoed horribly in the high, sunless space of the stairwell. Had Brown, God forbid, pulled the bell already? Had Alicia managed to signal her presence? Worse still, her plight?

'Robert! A fair surprise indeed!'

This is how villains manage, isn't it? They find within themselves, as I did that day on the stair, a faculty for splitting the world quite instantaneously into discrete compartments, uncoupling the awkward ones, shunting them temporarily from mind. The essence of integrity is wholeness, and wholeness precludes all self-deception, convenient black-outs, the expedient tossing of suddenly inconvenient factors into abeyance. Fail to hold everything in mind, and anything may happen: child-killers can come home at night and sweep their own daughters into fond cuddles; professional thieves can curse in the sincerest outrage to find their own cars gone from the kerb; and yes, yes, I openly admit it, a man like me can put distress, abuse, entirely out of thought and, turning into good fellowship itself, set milk and papers down on the door-mat and give Brown the glad hand, lay an arm round his shoulders and lead him off towards the nearest bar in an unwonted lather of cordiality. You'd think, if you'd been listening to our conversation as I ushered Brown before me through the swing doors, that I was entirely taken up with his new idea for the Honours courses. You'd think Alicia had ceased to exist. And you'd be right. Except in so far as she figured in a logistical problem – keeping the two of them well apart – I never gave the poor scrap a thought.

Naturally, somebody with a face like mine is not going to be fond of bars. They take a bit of stepping into. I'm generally twice unnerved: first by the sudden awed hiatus in the general hubbub as people glance in that automatic way towards the opening door and rising draught only to have the shock of seeing me; then by the almost instantaneous reprise of conversation so obviously born more of renascent courtesy than of any continuing interest in whatever topic was under discussion. Here in the Craggan Arms the second problem at least failed to arise. The moment the door swung open to reveal the two of us, dead silence fell. Two dozen men or more lifted their heads to stare at us. The silence lasted unbroken the time it took to thread our way between the wooden tables and benches to where the landlord stood behind the bar, spinning a glass on a cloth wrapped round his fingers, watching our approach.

Forgoing more ordinary domestic hospitality and stepping out instead for a pint had very clearly been my idea and not Brown's. This first round of drinks was definitely on me. So I leaned on the bar and made an effort. I'm never the sum and substance of sociability; but, on this occasion, from sheer discomposure I tended even more towards the brusque than usual. My request for two pints of Belhaven sounded a bit curmudgeonly even to my ears. Undeterred, though, the landlord reached behind him, and just as if he'd neither heard what I said nor registered the way I'd said it, he laid his large hands on tumblers and pulled some very dusty bottle of malt out from the back of a very low shelf. Ignoring all my attempts at protest, the fellow poured out two of the largest tots of whisky I ever saw a Scots landlord give any man. These he slammed on the counter between us, cheerfully announcing, 'On me. Ay, these two and the next.'

Behind and around, the tension of curiosity broke into loud astonishment. There were thuddings of beer-glasses on table tops and heavy foot stampings of approval. From the nearest table came the prompt heckle, 'How aboot us, then, Jamie?'

The other patrons nodded towards Brown and myself and grinned at the landlord, lifting their half-empty glasses and crowing, 'I wadna refuse another masel'!'

'Twa more here, Jamie. That's unco' guid o' ye!'

While I was wondering what sort of drinking place we'd happened into, the landlord stuck his hand out over the bar. He beamed. He chuckled. He shook my hand so enthusiastically that all the glasses between us rattled.

'It's certainly guid to meet ye, Professor Laidlaw.'

I simply stared.

Does everybody know who I am? At times like this, I could believe it.

'Professor Laidlaw, your very guid health!'

Now over the years I've come to terms with all the dearth of anonymity that comes with striking looks, fair or foul. I'm used to being noticed, covertly watched. I'm used to being unforgettable. I am accustomed to the fact that secretaries and receptionists never confuse me with other men, that if I leave a briefcase in a crowded bookshop, as soon as I return it's handed to me before I've even had time to explain that it's mine. However taciturn I am, however dull, no-one forgets me. I'm even used to people who went to conferences I attended over twenty years ago remembering me, and, more horrifically, the points I made, with crystal clarity. I've come to terms with all of this. Indeed I expect it. I even see it has its few advantages. I'm never held up, like Brown, at library checkpoints, scrabbling among the receipts in my wallet for some acceptable form of identification. No servitor ever queries my comings and goings, and no first-year student has ever caused me the common annoyance of standing shuffling in the half-open doorway, muttering inanely, 'I *think* it was you . . .'

But this, this was unparalleled. This was a horrible new twist, a staggering and most unwelcome refinement. I'd never before set foot in the place. To be known and known by name, where there's been no connection at all, neither professional nor personal, not even commercial . . .

Baffled, I raised my glass to his.

'And yours, Mr—?'

'Warner. James Allan Warner.'

The mouthful of whisky I took fair choked me.

So there it was. James Allan Warner. As decent-looking a father for young Warner as you could imagine. Large, frank and friendly, generous and trusting. Clearly a good and simple man, one whom at any other time I would be proud and pleased to know; but for the first time in a long teaching life I suddenly longed to be far from Scotland, employed more safely on the other side of the border, where students customarily choose universities as much for their healthy distance from home as for any educational advantage.

Clearly Brown entertained no such negative notions. He eyed his malt with pleasure, and raised his glass.

'Your very good health, Mr Warner. Your very good health. I've had the honour of teaching your son.'

'He's a quick laddie.'

'He certainly is.'

'Aye has his head buried in a book, that one.'

'Right. That's the way.'

I lifted my own glass and looked about as these two embarked upon this string of amiable pleasantries. I noticed with relief that, apart from the occasional inquisitive glance in my direction, all of James Allan Warner's regular patrons were settling back into serious drinking. And at this reminder of the supposedly tranquillizing properties of what I so shakily held in hand, I downed the whisky rather faster than usual.

No sooner had I emptied the tumbler than James Allan Warner refilled it to the brim.

'No. No. I am no drinker, really.'

'Awa' wi' ye!'

And I submitted. Certainly the malt was proving to have a most comforting effect. My hands stopped trembling. I breathed more easily. I realized suddenly how tired I had become, how shaken I'd been by all the stress of recent events. Leaving to Brown the task of larding our host with any further civilities necessary, I carried my whisky over to the far side of the room, ostensibly to examine four fly-blown prints hanging above the fireplace, in fact, after the most cursory of artistic inspections, to take the only cushioned chair in the room for my own.

I stretched out, glad for the warmth of fire on my legs and a few quiet moments in which to collect my thoughts and devise some inoffensive plan to uncouple myself from my colleague's companionship before returning to the flat. The last thing I wanted was Brown walking me home. Lord knows but how he might suddenly take it into his head to follow me up the stairs and borrow a book. It shouldn't prove too difficult to think of some reason to start us walking in his direction, not mine, before parting. Meeting a train? I might get into awkward talk of timetables. Luncheon engagement? He might ask civilly with whom. I combed my scattered wits for other, less perilous, excuses. Nothing came to mind. But if I did close my eyes against the fire's comforting flicker, it wasn't so much the press of thought as the fact that the pall of tobacco smoke hanging about this poorly ventilated drinking place stung my eyes. But it must have appeared to my neighbours as if I had promptly fallen asleep. Certainly the two old men behind my chair dropped their voices lower, so that their fragments of chat became barely audible through my fog of exhaustion. And maybe I did doze off for just a short while. Certainly I have no recollection of how it began, that strange, desultory conversation overheard.

'His faither said it: Aye had his head buried in a book.'

'And aye a guid conceit o' himself!'

I heard the ancient bench they shared begin to creak. Were they rocking together in gentle amusement? After a pause, the gruffer of the two voices picked up the theme.

'Granting us all a grand favour in going tae the university.'

'And himsel' twa more!'

More creaking, followed by 'I'm no so certain o' that masel'. I reckon that clever lassie o' his has had an eye for another this while back.'

'Probably awa' wi' the other this minute. The wee stories! Workin' the nights! Off hame every weekend! Och, awa'! The things a woman will expect ye to believe, if ye live long enough!'

'It's out o' thocht that she's the one who's payin' for all these telephone calls . . .'

Telephone calls . . . telephone calls . . . A vision of my own last inexplicably costly bill swam in the darkness behind my closed eyes. Seventy-one pounds. Seventy-one pounds! Had she some tender confidante in Tasmania?

Some old boyfriend helping sink wells in Bihar? I'd never had a phone bill like it. Even Margaret, in the last few weeks of our union when she was in, I suspect, almost constant contact with my successor, forbore from landing me with such a bill as that. I'm sure, to be fair, that Alicia was no worse in this respect than many of her peers. It falls squarely on them to keep communication technology one of the few growth industries in the declining economy. Not at their own expense, of course: always at someone else's, the prudent and restrained phone-after-sixers whose lack of spontaneity they so despise. According to Brown, such wastefulness is perfectly normal. Excessive and inconsiderate use of the phone is, he maintains, the first clear sign of female puberty. But seventy-one pounds! I stirred uncomfortably in the chair, and maybe to furnish consolation there floated up from depths of memory some other ancient story of Brown's about the first and last sherry party he ever laid on for his students, a merry if brief occasion on which nineteen young men and women consumed in just under an hour and a half what the man in the off-licence assured Brown would last three such parties.

Behind me, the two old codgers still harped and carped.

'He's gone fair shuttle-witted, if ye ask me.'

'Och, weel. Trail a wing the laddie may, but it'll no be him that has the keepin' o' her in the end.'

I could have chimed in, 'And lucky to escape!' But was my experience anything to go by? Might it not be pure cynicism speaking? Worse, cynicism born of excess? No. No, not that. What they'd have heard from me was tired middle-age, worn ragged from its tangle with youth. I'd warn an enemy off taking them up. They're terrifying. Appalling in their sheer profligacy. Watch them, the young, the still-immortals, frittering away their aeons of time and quantities of energy to no real purpose except that of growing older. Fall in with that lot at your peril. You'll squander your own more limited resources, and still only keep up with them for so long. In the end you must, if you are sane, be unnerved.

'To think on how she holds the stick o'er the twa o' them!'

To think on it indeed. And why not? It was, as Brown would say, perfectly normal. Why shouldn't a pretty lassie dabble a bit? She'd made no promises to any husband had she? She'd brought no children into the world for whose sake she should be trying to lead a responsible life. If she'd the energy to run two lovers at a time, good luck to her from this old crock whose stuffing fell out from just managing one.

'I wadna' say but what there'll be a fell stramash one day between the two laddies, to see which'll get her . . .'

Well, not on my account, there wouldn't. She'd get no fell stramash from me. I'd rather help her pack and lend her the bus fare. Give her a kiss, thank her for everything and wish her good luck with the other fellow. At the mere thought of it, my body softened and relaxed, my spirits lifted. Was it simply the whisky making me mellow? Or was it more that only now, outside the stifling confines of my own flat, and here, beside these rusty ancients wheezing out their passionless counterpoint of 'seen it before' and 'what does it matter?', could I see all the grisly boiling for what it was: simply the end of an affair? Letting love go is more of a skill than finding it, after all. And when a woman has to leave, she should be furnished with the wherewithal to sail out in dignity and confidence, not creep out looking and feeling like a wee bird with all its little feathers pulled off.

'It's aye the bonnie anes that make your hair staun up on end.'

'The lassie's neither to haud nor to bind!'

To hold . . . to bind . . . Oh God! Alicia! Alicia! Held, bound, in such distress, and all my fault, all done by me! I must be mad, to think that I could set up such a scheme to rid myself of inconvenience, and cause her one small ounce of misery. What had I done? Making her suffer for my advantage! What had sweet, idle, easy-going Alicia ever done to me, for God's own sake, that I should punish her like this? It was monstrous.

I felt quite sick. The barbarous plan I had conceived was, only half a mile away, hatching into something foul and real to cause me everlasting shame. Couldn't it be stopped? Spinning the empty tumbler off the chair arm, I leaped to my feet. The crash of glass shattering on stone flags alerted everyone to my frenzied arousal. Brown swivelled his head in my direction, and even James Allan Warner halted his stolid, rhythmic wiping of glass to stare across the room at me. Indeed, everyone stared. But I'd no time to stop, and there are more important things than courtesies and explanations. I rushed for the doorway, knocking against the backs of chairs and edges of tables, and even stumbling over carelessly splayed limbs not drawn back fast enough by the astonished customers as I fought past them. I threw my weight full on the door. A pane of coloured glass split under the heel of my hand with a gunfire report, but I pushed through, and as the door crashed back against the wall the fragments splintered and showered everywhere. I ran out, half blinded by sudden slanting winter sunlight, over one street and into another, cutting in front of startled car-drivers and disapproving Sunday strollers who snatched their unsteady infants hastily aside. I ran faster and faster, panting and moaning with the exertion, desperate to reach Alicia and set her free, throw myself at her poor, cold, bare feet and on her mercy, beg her forgiveness, kiss away the tears, bathe her and soothe her and make it all better. Get back inside the flat, and stop it. Make it as though it all never had been.

Chapter 12

The silence of some people is worse than swearing. This time she didn't turn her head away from me as I came in. I wish she had. I stumbled through the door and leaned flat back against it, heaving and gasping. My head swirled viciously from the whisky. My throat burned. Every limb shook uncontrollably. And as I struggled to haul my body back into some semblance of restraint, those eyes, those unforgettable dark stains in the pale face, were watching, watching.

'Oh, don't,' I begged, as soon as I had breath enough. 'Shut your eyes, *please*.'

It was as though she didn't hear. I had to stagger to the bedside and lay my hand across her eyes, to stop her.

'Sssh!' I said. 'Sssh!'

I used the other hand to release her. Reaching across the chill little body, I slid the catches on the metal figures of-eight – simple for me, impossible for her – freeing her limbs. She couldn't move. It was quite clear she couldn't move. I had to take her arms and lift them round. They felt so stiff, like little wooden sticks, I thought that they might snap in my hand. Around her wrists weals shone, raw and bloody, as though her two hands were still somehow loosely tied with frayed but glossy scarlet ribbons. I pushed her cold, splayed legs a little closer together, for decency's sake. Beneath them, the bed-sheet was damp and stained and sharp-smelling. I never saw a sight more pitiful.

'Alicia, my love . . .'

Sliding my arm around her, I pulled her up. The sudden movement caused her to cry in pain. Her eyes snapped open in that strange, unnerving way dolls' eyes snap open and closed, like shutters. These were no empty doll's eyes, though. Inside them, little coals were burning.

'Don't look at me,' I begged her. 'Be kind.'

My plea had no effect. I pushed Brightmony off the pillows piled up beside her and thrust them, one by one, behind her back. When I let go her body slid, inflexible and indifferent, as far down as their sagging permitted. And there she lay, unresponsive and silent.

I pushed the hair back from her face. She barely blinked. I pulled a handkerchief out of my pocket.

'Here, spit!' I ordered her, holding it underneath her chin. She didn't smile. I might as well have made the joke in Serbo-Croat for all the recognition it received: not a flicker.

Folding the handkerchief into neat quarters, I dipped a corner in the glass of stale water beside me. I rubbed at the grime and dried tears on her face. She watched me for all the world as if the filthy mess at which I scrubbed so gently was nothing whatsoever to do with her, and I was attending to someone else entirely.

I couldn't stand it.

'Alicia,' I warned, 'don't look at me this way. I'm not a monster.'

As if to prove the point, a surge of such contrition rose in me that I was suddenly filled with desire, and desire all the more urgent after so many weeks of stolidly nurtured indifference. For all her dirty face and pallid, unfeeling body, for all the bed-sheet beneath was damp and disgusting, I wanted her, and wanted her badly. She must have known. She must have seen the look in my eyes, and recognized it for what it was. She had her eyes wide open. She saw. She must have perceived my love and known that all I wanted was to cherish her, for she was still my greatest treasure.

I bent to kiss her. I leaned across to lay the soft and gentle proof of my remorse and tenderness upon her lips.

And now she spat. Spat with such force of loathing that I was shocked – deeply, deeply shocked.

Slowly and carefully, I unfolded the damp and soiled handkerchief and found a clean patch. I wiped the thin string of her spittle from my chin.

'I understand', I told her, 'that you are justifiably over-wrought. None the less, that was a hurtful and repellent gesture.'

She burst into hysterical tears. I'm not insensitive. I instantly regretted my harshness of tone. I bent to try to comfort her, but she had lost her senses entirely.

Shuddering quite uncontrollably, she plastered her palms over her eye-sockets, and shrieked, 'Take your foul face away from me!'

Now this did annoy me. With not quite so much restraint as I'd been showing up till now, I prised the heels of her hands away from her eyes. Taking her chin firmly between my fingers, I pulled her towards me and reminded her, 'You got enough of a charge out of it once, didn't you, my precious?'

She thrashed and fought to free herself, but still I wouldn't let up. I held her so tightly by the chin that the lower half of her face was contorted. I thrust my face right up against her own.

'Open your eyes.'

She struggled desperately.

'Open your eyes!'

I slapped her breasts, one after the other, hard as I could, ordering her levelly, word by word, slap by vicious slap, 'Open – your – eyes – open – your – eyes – open—'

Until they opened. And now a tremor ran through her, a flinching and a shrinking of such disgust, such revulsion, that you'd have thought the blood ran cold inside her veins, and for one quite extraordinary moment her face appeared even more distorted to me than my own.

I let go of her poor, bruised chin. She cradled it between her fingers, making a little noise to herself, a kind of high, demented, chattering hum. The only sense I managed to make of it was at the end when she looked up and whispered, 'You know what you are, Ian Laidlaw?'

I sat back, waiting.

'You're ugly, you are. So ugly.'

She said it with wonder, with reverence almost. You'd think she might have been admiring me, the way that she came out with it.

'You are an ugly man, inside and out.'

'Yes,' I said. 'Yes.'

And no-one ever guessed, before her. No-one. Why should they? No-one begins to try to guess at what's behind deformities and scars. We people are a race apart. It is the fault of people like you. You keep us that way, after all. You stay behind your bulwarks of unfailing politeness. You don't engage. And so we are habitually permitted, encouraged one might even say, to use our various hideous blemishes as scapegoats to save ourselves from having to admit to other weaknesses. What other weaknesses? Who knows? Shallowness? Spite? All manner of emotional disablement. All sorts of failings. We are all individuals after all. I can speak only for myself.

Alicia knew, though. As I slipped off my jacket and hung it with care over the back of the chair, the accusation came.

'You're vicious, you are. Like that dog.'

I loosened the knot of my tie.

'Which dog, sweetheart?'

'Which dog! The dog that tore your face into that mess!'

I draped the tie over the jacket.

'That dog wasn't so very vicious. Over that wall I'd been tormenting him for months.'

'Like you've tormented me!'

I whipped the leather belt out of my trousers.

'It could be argued there are similarities.'

'Ian!' She started weeping. 'Why, Ian? *Why*?'

I tugged at the zip of my trousers.

'Alicia, Alicia,' I sighed. 'Such sloppy questions! When will your education ever take?'

Credit where credit's due, she made no effort to get away as I pulled off my shirt and started in. She knew when she was beaten. There was no point. I would have hung her up by the heels sooner than let her wriggle out of this, the fruit of forty years of civilized restraint. I pushed her back and let her have it. And as I took the belt to her, I was for the first time in my life ruthlessly and entirely my own man, the whole man she had made of me. My face burned, all of it, and it burned hard. All of me burned. Not just one half of me, the pleasant half that's all poor Margaret ever knew, the half I've always shown the rest of you, the half you rocks always insisted on seeing. All the rest, too. She had got through. It filled me with wonder, but she had done it. She'd managed what no-one else has ever managed: she'd got through to me in the only way there is, the way I'd warned her all those months ago, when I first took her by the wrists and shook her and told her, 'Understand this, little Alicia. To get to me you have to go in through the scar patch here. There isn't any other way.' She'd done it, as I'd somehow known she could, right from the day when, in that seminar, she first laughed in my face.

She'd let the ugly side of me loose. I beat down on the cringing and the whimpering, and felt the stiff, stiff gristle of scar-tissue giving, as muscles I hadn't even known my face possessed began to stir. I was, I realized in some shock, grinning. Whole at last, I was think-ing. Whole at last. What won't I now be free to show her?

And it was anger. Bursting from me, the adder ready for release after a wait of over forty years. Anger, the gift I gave her, felt with a force I never could have believed would be mine. Anger. I split with it as I split her with it. It ran all over me as it ran over her, through me and her, eviscerating, spilling and emptying. I let it go. I felt as if I were exploding, as if the meretricious little bitch had somehow sprung some secret catch in me, exposing my core as I now raised a sweat exposing hers, laying bare all that lay hidden for years under the cover of my scar patch just as I now laid bare for her all that lay hidden under that soft, red and bloody puddle of skin.

I will not tell you all I did to her. I doubt if she, if she were here, would want it told. I have no reason to 'con-fess the worst' to you. I seek no expiation, just as I expect to get no forgiveness. I loved her and I killed her. That should be clear enough. You go off home tonight and run your fingers along your bookshelves, looking for *Mind of the Murderer* or *Male Sexual Violence*. Flick through your ancient police college notes. Ask your wife, even. You'll surely manage to come up with some explanation for all I felt and all I did. But stay away from me with your facile conclusions. I'm a whole man, and will not be diminished by any glib psychology of yours. I loved her and I killed her. But not so fast! You listen here.

It was an accident.

Well may your eyebrows shoot up through the ceiling. I say again, I killed Alicia purely by accident, and I dare

213

you, after my more than scrupulous truthfulness, to doubt one single word I say.

The doorbell rang. Oh, yes, it did! Ask Brown. Ask Brown! Ask the invertebrate weakling how long it took him to cover the little more than half a mile from the Craggan Arms to my street, how long it took him to get up the stairs, how long he stood outside the door in doubt and gathering anxiety, before he put his fingers around the bell-pull and tugged.

He must have heard her scream. The whole world must. I shoved the pillow over her face, but not before she'd made the ceiling and walls ring with it. Such a scream! I've heard it echo in my ears ever since.

You know what it's like when a woman struggles. For one short, blind moment I pressed harder. That's all, I swear it. One short, short moment. No more than a couple of seconds, at most. It was not possible that she suffocated. No-one could suffocate in such a short while. It wasn't even as if she weakened. One moment she was struggling under me with all the fierceness that panic allows, next moment she was limp as damp cloth. I whipped the pillow off. I was astonished. Only the slightest blush around her face gave one to think she was anything but sleeping. I've read my share of thrillers. I know what suffocation's supposed to look like, and I tell you that I could not have suffocated her. Impossible. Impossible.

Did I try what? No. No, I didn't. It may have been remiss of me, but though it crossed my mind I somehow didn't like to try, in case it failed.

What then . . . ? I beg your pardon, I was miles away . . . What then?

First, I got dressed. Then I turned down the thermostat on the radiator. I turned it down as far as it would go, and opened the window. I didn't open it so much that people opposite would notice and wonder; just a couple of inches at top and bottom. Enough, at this time of year, to stir up a draught and chill the room thoroughly.

I pulled one of the sheets I very rarely use from the bottom of the pile in the airing cupboard, and spread it out, over the bed. It somehow didn't do the job it was supposed to do – it was too thin – and so I had to go back and dig out another to lay on top. Margaret's soft spot for bright colours tended always to come out worst in sheets, and I confess to finding the effect of the two strongly contrasting patterns garish and off-putting.

I gathered the duvet up from the floor and carried it through into the living-room. I dumped it down on the settee. Then I stood for a couple of minutes trying to work out exactly what I needed to take from the bedroom – fresh shirt, socks, a couple of books on the floor by the bed, that sort of thing. I went back in and fetched everything I thought I possibly might need. Then I took one last look around, shooed Brightmony out in front of me, and closed the door with some relief.

I spent the evening at my desk. There was a lot to get through. The letters to the Dean and Principal took hardly any time. A resignation note is pretty standard, however singular the reason behind it. The other letters took more time. At first I tried to write to Alicia's parents jointly. This proved impossible, and after an hour or more of frustration I tore up the envelope addressed to them both, and wrote separate letters to each, instead. The one to her father is, you may have noticed, uncomfortably formal. It was the best that I could do. What I wrote to her mother is, I hope, a little more human. It cannot comfort now, but it may later. I hope you'll make no difficulties, and send them on.

The letter to Margaret was by far the longest. It runs to several pages of requests and advice and instructions about about my personal affairs and effects. I have it here. I carry it about because I keep thinking of other things to add. Unravelling a lifetime is quite a business. Most of it I expect her to put straight into the hands of a solicitor. But there are some matters – the storage of my grandmother's nice bits and pieces, for example – that I think she'll probably take upon herself. I hope so, anyway. Margaret has always proved a rock, and I'd be easier in mind to think that she was acting for my interests. It isn't such an imposition. Those bits and pieces are not only mostly rather nice, they're valuable too. She's going to have them on very long loan, and possibly for ever. It's all willed to her anyway, in the event of my own death. It always has been. Since there was no-one else to make my beneficiary after she left, I never bothered to change my will, except to scrub out the word 'wife' and put instead her strange new name.

I spent the night on the sofa. It may seem monstrous of me, but I slept well, and only woke to sunlight in my eyes and Brightmony fussing and scratching and yowling for food.

I would have carried him over to a strange part of the city and left him there to fend for himself; but it didn't seem right. He'd been an indoor cat for quite some time now, and was, I suspected, far too old and spoiled to make it in the big bad world. I didn't, by the same token, like the idea of him being caged up in one of those cat homes indefinitely awaiting adoption. So I drowned him. I put him in one of the more gaudy pillowcases and drowned him in the bath. It took some time, though I'm sure in my determination to be thorough I held him under for far longer than necessary. I drained the water from the pillowcase without looking inside, and dropped the whole heavy, wet lump into a black plastic garbage bag. I took it straight down to the street, thinking myself fortunate that refuse collection quite recently changed to Mondays on the street where I live. By the time I went past again, on my way in to work, the bag had gone.

I reached the office early, before the secretaries, and slid the little white slip from the Health Centre in between two typed letters in the in-tray. I knew the slip was sorely out of date, but I didn't think it mattered. Usually no-one but me looks closely at these things, and the whole thing was, in any event, only a bit of a gamble for one or two extra days for my own convenience. Word gets around, and I knew that as soon as Warner took it into his head to play at Florence Nightingale, and found her missing from her flat, your lot would be called along in a jiffy. I expect I'll have my critics for taking these last couple of days of freedom. What can I say? I made the most of them. I fobbed off Brown, when he peered closely in my face and embarked upon a few inept and

217

stumbling words of concern. I set my examination questions for all my courses. I marked piles of essays. I cleared my desk of all the correspondence that had banked up. I left a long and detailed memorandum on all outstanding departmental matters for my successor, and left a note inside Scott-Watson's official file strongly recommending his ousting from the honours programme at the first opportunity that might present itself to my erstwhile colleagues. I tidied up my papers, and emptied the top drawer of my desk of small personal items, which I carried home at the end of the day.

I walked back home across the park, reflecting as usual, trying to take stock. The affair, I knew from the start, could not end in marriage; and if not in marriage, then what else can an affair ever end in, except pain and disaster, loss and tears? Life is no fairy tale, and this was not a story of Beauty and Beast, with their eventual triumph over ugliness. I proved to have none of Beast's gentleness and nobility of mind, and there were aspects of Alicia that mesh most uncomfortably with one's notion of Beauty. None the less, I felt wretched. Waste is still waste, for all its sick and sorry inevitability.

I spent that evening and the next cleaning – must we go on with this? Haven't I told you everything you need to know, and more, much more? Must you know *everything*? How, when the faintly rotten smell began to seep out under the door, I shoved a rug hard up against the gap, and kept on vacuuming and kept on vacuuming? How, last night, I finally ran out of things to do, and so came here to spend the night in my desk chair and wake dishevelled and exhausted, to meet the cleaners? How

Brown and the secretaries kept tormenting me, telling me to go back off home to my bed! How I could not and would not. How happy and relieved I was, standing and staring through this window here, to see you and your henchmen walk this way across the lawns, and know that it was over, all over. How, from sheer nerves, I sat down at my desk and started fiddling with pen and paper, acting important and busy, until you knocked.

Can we go now? I'm very tired.

THE END

TELLING LIDDY

Anne Fine

'BEAUTIFULLY WRITTEN, COMPULSIVELY READABLE . . . A CLEVER NOVELIST AT THE HEIGHT OF HER POWERS'
Independent

The Palmer sisters are close. They see each other often, they care for one another's children and houses and pets. They lend each other books, spare heaters and clothes for special occasions. Their phones ring in a ceaseless chat about in-laws and job plans and anxieties and triumphs. They never keep any secrets from each other – until now.

Stella tells Bridie a rumour she's heard about Liddy's new boyfriend. Bridie is shocked, and discusses it with Heather. But should they tell Liddy, and risk ruining her new-found happiness? Bridie persuades her sisters that they should, but when Liddy reacts badly, the other two backslide and Bridie becomes the outcast, bereft of the sisterly support system on which she has based her whole life.

'ANNE FINE WRITES WITH THE TOUCH OF AN AVENGING ANGEL: FLAWLESS PROSE, PERFECT PITCH, AND A FOLLOW-THROUGH THAT KNOCKS THE WIND FROM YOUR LUNGS'
Scotland on Sunday

'THIS LIVELY, FUNNY NOVEL IS ONE OF THOSE BOOKS THAT MAKES YOU WINCE WITH DELIGHT AT, AND HORRIFIED RECOGNITION OF, ANNE FINE'S TALENT AT PEELING AWAY OUR CAREFULLY MAINTAINED IDEAS OF OURSELVES'
Observer

'HUGELY ENJOYABLE AND DISTURBINGLY ACUTE'
Mail on Sunday

'HER COPIOUS AND OFTEN COMICAL DIALOGUE RINGS ENTIRELY TRUE (A RARE GIFT), WHILE OUT OF THE EPHEMERA OF EVERYDAY LIFE SHE CONSTRUCTS A TALE OF LASTING POWER; FINE LIVES UP TO HER NAME'
Financial Times

0 552 99770 6

BLACK SWAN

TAKING THE DEVIL'S ADVICE

Anne Fine

'A BRILLIANTLY ORCHESTRATED SLANGING-
MATCH'
Independent

Spending the summer with his ex-wife, his children, his ex-
gardener (and ex-wife's new husband) was never going to be a
good idea.

Perhaps Oliver should have expected the autobiography he
was writing to be constantly sabotaged? Perhaps he should
have guessed that he'd have scorn and derision poured upon
him? But then Oliver was a philosopher, always happier with
abstraction than reality and the realities of his life have never
been simple. Now they're about to come crashing down
around him in the most unexpected and hilarious of ways.

'ANNE FINE'S BLACK COMEDY BOUNCES ALONG
ITS SPRIGHTLY ONE-LINERS WITHOUT FLAGGING'
Observer

'SHOT THROUGH WITH WIT, AND FULL OF
EFFERVESCENCE AND GOOD HUMOUR'
Financial Times

'IT IS SAID TO TAKE TWO TO MAKE A QUARREL
BUT THE *CASUS BELLI* FOR CONSTANCE AFTER
SIXTEEN YEARS OF MARRIAGE IS HER
PHILOSOPHER HUSBAND OLIVER'S SERENE
UNAWARENESS OF EVER HAVING GIVEN
GROUNDS FOR ONE . . . CLEVER AND
ENTERTAINING . . . A DIRELY WITTY
ACHIEVEMENT'
Guardian

'ALIVE WITH BRAZEN CHARM'
Mail on Sunday

0 552 99826 5

BLACK SWAN

IN COLD DOMAIN

Anne Fine

'A SEXY, VIOLENT, MERVYN PEAKE-ISH FABLE OF
FAMILY LIFE'
New Statesman

Like her legendary namesake, Lilith Collett lives in an Eden
she is bent on destroying. If her family vex or thwart her in
any way, the paradise of a garden that enchanted their
childhood suffers for it. The vine, the rockery, the pergola –
nothing at Cold Domain is safe from Lilith's ruthless slash-
and-burn policy. Enter an archangel: Miguel-Angel Arqueso
Algarón Perez de Vega, under whose spell downtrodden
Barbara dares defy her mother. And when William's lover
Caspar also joins the battle in his own subtle way, the fate of
the Colletts and their garden are finally and unexpectedly
sealed.

'A STREAMLINED, RUTHLESSLY STRIPPED-DOWN
PSYCHOLOGICAL FAMILY ROMANCE WITH
ENOUGH PLOT TWISTS AND CHARACTER
REVELATIONS TO FUEL A BOOK THREE TIMES AS
LONG. WICKED AND FUNNY. ANNE FINE
IS BRILLIANT'
Time Out

'SWOOPING GRACEFULLY FROM SERIOUSNESS TO
FARCE AND BACK AGAIN, ANNE FINE SUCCEEDS
IN EXPOSING A WHOLE GAMUT OF HIDDEN
EMOTIONS IN AN ADMIRABLY PERCEPTIVE NOVEL'
Good Housekeeping

'A GLORIOUS TIRADE AGAINST THE GRIND OF
MOTHERHOOD'
Observer

0 552 99827 3

BLACK SWAN

A SELECTED LIST OF FINE WRITING AVAILABLE FROM BLACK SWAN

THE PRICES SHOWN BELOW WERE CORRECT AT THE TIME OF GOING TO PRESS. HOWEVER TRANSWORLD PUBLISHERS RESERVE THE RIGHT TO SHOW NEW RETAIL PRICES ON COVERS WHICH MAY DIFFER FROM THOSE PREVIOUSLY ADVERTISED IN THE TEXT OR ELSEWHERE.

All Transworld titles are available by post from:

Book Services By Post, P.O. Box 29, Douglas, Isle of Man IM99 1BQ

Credit cards accepted. Please telephone 01624 675137,
fax 01624 670923 or Internet http://www.bookpost.co.uk.
or e-mail: bookshop@enterprise.net for details

Free postage and packing in the UK. Overseas customers: allow
£1 per book (paperbacks) and £3 per book (hardbacks).